HIS FIANCÉ TO KEEP

A BILLIONAIRE FAKE FIANCÉ ROMANCE

HAPPILY EVER BILLIONAIRES
BOOK THREE

VIVIAN WOOD

AUTHOR'S COPYRIGHT

HIS FIANCÉ TO KEEP

1

***

SAM

"*I* don't care if the peonies bloomed late this year!" Sam said in exasperation to the florist on the other end of the line. "And the client certainly isn't going to care. You're going to have to find them from somewhere because I expect sixty arrangements ready by Friday afternoon."

"And where do you think I'm going to get sixty arrangements in three days?" the florist snapped back. "Trust me, American Beauty roses are a perfectly acceptable replacement. I don't make the seasons, honey."

Sam groaned and tucked her dark hair behind her ears. *This job is a freaking nightmare. Since when did planning parties mean going to battle daily with idiot vendors?* "It's not my job to figure out where the flowers come from. That's your job," she said slowly.

"Look, you're an event manager," the florist said. "Manage it, because I'm not going to work a miracle and pull a dozen fully blossomed peony bushes out of my ass."

"Listen, pretty much everything else has gone wrong with this banquet so far, and I'm not going to tell the client that they're not going to get the flowers they paid thousands of dollars for the week of the event."

"I don't know who you think you are," the florist said. "And I've certainly never heard of you, and I've been working with your company for ten years. You must be new."

"I've been here six months," Sam said.

"Well, that explains a lot," the florist laughed.

Sam rolled her eyes and caught a glimpse of a gorgeous blond walking through the door. He was built like a machine, broad chest and shoulders. She remembered him from sitting in on his consultation appointment weeks ago. *Connor, that's it. He was getting married in a few months—lucky bitch.* Through her glass office walls, she watched him as he looked around the office, until finally Jenny—the event coordinator assigned to his account—scrambled up to him.

"Are you there?" the florist asked.

"Yes. Are you getting the peonies?" she replied. Jenny was flustered, and Connor rubbed his temples. She watched as he dropped his head into his hands and began to shout at Jenny. From the other side of the room, she couldn't make out what was being said.

"…Beauty roses are of a higher quality, so I'll need an additional payment…"

"I'm going to have to call you back," Sam said.

"Are you kidding me?"

Sam hung up the phone and made a beeline for Jenny and the guy. *Connor is the hottest guy I've ever seen,* she thought. And that counted the male models she hung out with on the regular. They were gorgeous, of course, but so svelte and fragile looking. Connor looked like he could pin her up against the wall and keep her there.

"I'm really sorry," Jenny said to Connor. Her voice trembled. "But the order has already been placed with the florist—"

"Is something wrong?" Sam asked. "Can I help?"

"Yes, something's wrong," Connor said to her curtly. "And I doubt you can help, but why don't you give it a go? My fiancée cheated on me, so this five-thousand-dollar deposit *I* put down on this godforsaken wedding needs to be charged to my ex and her family."

"Oh," Sam said. Her mouth snapped shut. She hadn't expected this.

"I tried to tell him—" Jenny started.

Sam brushed her away. "I'll take care of this," she said. "Hi, my name's Sam. We met briefly during your consultation." She reached out and shook Connor's hand. It was huge and callused on the palms from weightlifting. She swallowed hard.

"I'm not trying to be rude here, but I don't have time for these niceties," he said. "All I want is this mess to be over with and to not get stuck with thousands of dollars worth of flowers and cake." He looked down at her, and his steely blue eyes bored through her.

"I, I understand," she stammered.

"Do you? Are you married, engaged?" he asked.

"Well, no—"

"Then how in the hell can you understand?" he asked.

Her face burned. "I've been cheated on before," she murmured. She felt the eyes of her colleagues shoot toward her, even as they pretended to be hard at work at their desks.

"We've all been cheated on," he said. "It's a little different when your credit card is involved, and you just walked in on your fiancée with some guy's dick in her mouth."

From behind Connor's shoulder, Jenny watched and her eyes bugged out.

"I, um, I guess you're right," Sam said. "Look, let me go talk to my boss for just a moment. Why don't you come wait in my office, and I'll smooth things over?" As she led him toward her glass enclosure, she could swear she felt his eyes on her ass. She couldn't help but put a little extra swing in her hips.

"This you?" he asked, looking around her sleek office with a view of the Pentagon. "Fancy."

She blushed. "I'll be right back. Help yourself to some water if you'd like."

Sam hustled toward her boss' office at the other end of the building. "He's hot!" Jenny said as she flew by.

She knocked at the door. "What do you need?" Mrs. Whiteworth called from the other side.

"Mrs. Whiteworth, it's Sam. I have a situation."

"Come in." The owner of the company sighed and put her glasses on the mahogany desk. "Yes, what disaster has struck now? Did someone's fondant cake show up with whipped buttercream instead?"

"Um, no," Sam said. "There's a client here and he… well, he caught his fiancée cheating on him and he wants the deposit he put down for their wedding transferred to her and her family."

"When was the wedding?"

"I don't know." Mrs. Whiteworth frowned.

"Have any of the orders been placed?"

"I don't know."

"It seems like there's a lot you don't know. And why, may I ask, don't you know these details if you're planning this hot little mess?"

"Well, actually, Jenny is the planner. But he was flipping out on her so I'm trying to help—"

"Sticking your nose where it doesn't belong," Mrs. Whiteworth said.

Sam looked down, embarrassed.

"Sometimes that's what it takes to get the job done. I'll have a talk with Jenny later. That girl needs to grow some balls. But given that the wedding is pretty far out and I'm in a generous mood, tell him I'll go ahead and bill the girl. Just make sure he doesn't leave without getting her full contact information, including address."

"Yes, ma'am," Sam said, looking at her boss with a smile.

"This wouldn't happen to be the Harris account, would it?" she asked.

"Harris?"

"What was the boy's name... oh, yes, Connor," she said, leaning back in her plush leather chair.

"Yes, it is. Why?" Sam asked.

Mrs. Whiteworth smiled knowingly. "I might be well seasoned, sweetheart, but I'm not dead. He's a dream, and Jenny's apparently flailing about like some school-girl with a crush."

"Yes, ma'am," she said.

"Oh, cut the ma'am crap and get back to Mr. Universe. Tell him he doesn't have to worry about paying for it."

"Thank you," Sam said, smiling sweetly and shutting the door behind her. As she hurried back to her office, she could barely contain her excitement.

"Well?" Jenny asked her as she cut her off at the water fountain.

"It's fine, don't worry about it," she said. Jenny clasped her chest and smiled gratefully.

Connor looked up at her when she walked in. He had one of the small lollipops she kept on her desk tucked into his cheek. "You got good news for me?" he asked, although it sounded like more of a command.

"Good news," she said with a grin. "The boss approved a transfer. I'll just need to get your fiancée's contact information. Ex-fiancée," she corrected herself. "Then we can—"

"You know what? Never mind. It doesn't matter."

"Never mind?" *Had he miraculously reconciled with his ex while she'd been going to bat for him with the scariest boss ever?*

"I have a proposal for you. But it would be outside the company's… purview, if you will." He leaned against her desk, thick arms crossed over his chest.

"Um, I'm not sure I know what you mean? Do you—do you still want me to transfer the invoice?"

He shrugged, nonchalant. "Do what you like in that regard, I'm done messing with it. But here's what I do want you to do. Meet me for a drink later today."

"A drink?" She was suddenly uncertain what to do with her hands. Sam pulled at her skintight skirt and readjusted the hem of her jacket.

"You know, a drink," he said. "You, me, a bar of my choosing. What do you say?" He pulled the candy out from between his lips.

"Um, yes. Yeah, sure," she said. "That sounds good."

Connor looked her up and down, unabashedly. She felt his eyes crawl over the swell of her calves, linger at the splay of her hips and travel to her waist. He took in the curve of her breasts, the hollow of her throat and finally met her gaze—and held it for an uncomfortable amount of time. He nodded to himself, then turned and took a pen and pad of paper from her desk.

"Here's the time, place, and my number," he said as he tore off the piece of paper. He walked toward her and she gulped. "Don't be late," he said.

When he handed her the slip of paper, their hands touched and it was electric.

Connor left, and Sam along with the entire office watched his departure. *What have you gotten yourself into now?*

"Oh my God," Jenny said as soon as he was swallowed by the elevator. "What was that? What happened?"

"I don't—I'm not sure," she said honestly.

"What's that?" Jenny asked, and she snatched the paper out of Sam's hand. "The Rye Bar? Sam, what's going on? Did he… did he ask you out? Are you going?"

"Jenny, be quiet," Sam said softly.

"Sam! C'mon, you have to tell me. That was the weirdest, and hottest, thing I've ever experienced. So are you going or not? Is it tonight?"

"I don't think I really have a choice," Sam said. Connor had been so sure, so confident, like he never doubted for a second that she wouldn't jump at the chance to go out with him.

"What do you mean? Sam, did he threaten you? Oh my God, I'll never forgive myself if he—"

"Jenny, for goodness' sake, he didn't threaten me! I… yes, it's tonight, and yes I'm going."

"Oh!" Jenny pretended to fan herself. "Dang, I wish I would have kept it together. Then maybe he would have asked me out. What are you going to wear?"

"I don't know. This? I don't think I have time to go home and change."

"Don't be stupid! Go buy something on your lunch break, get a Brazilian blowout—get a Brazilian *wax*, you crazy girl. You gotta make the most of tonight."

Sam bit her lip and grinned at Jenny. "Maybe you're right," she said.

CONNOR

He waited at the bar and sipped on his Dalmore scotch. The rich wood paneling complemented the long stretch of the bar. Couples were draped over one another, men with wedding band tans on their fingers hungered over girls barely old enough to drink, and flocks of single girls teetered in stilettos. He'd always loved this place. You could be anybody here.

Connor smirked to himself. It had only taken him a few minutes after seeing Sam to hatch his plan. He knew his father was going to cut him off as soon as he heard about the broken wedding—that was part of the deal. Connor got the COO position as soon as he got married. And as far as his father was concerned, an engagement with a set date was as good as married.

But now? It didn't matter that the paperwork had been signed. His father could make that paperwork disappear in a second.

What Connor needed was a decoy. A fake fiancée. A girl who would answer to the name Sandra and never get caught with some other guy's dick in her mouth — because she would be getting paid to play the role. Then, he could still get the business and claim the proverbial throne he'd been promised.

Now all he had to do was get Sam to agree to it.

He saw her enter through the mirrored back of the bar. She was a knockout, it was clear, even from across the room. The huddles of single men craned their necks in unison, and even the men cooing with their lovers looked up to drink her in. *Maybe it wasn't the best idea to choose a girl simply because she was stunning,* he thought to himself.

Sam caught sight of him, waved, and started to make her way through the crowd. *But she has a real job, too.* That would please his father. For once, he was grateful his father had never asked any details about Sandra besides whether or not she belonged to the country club. That would mean less lies to remember with Sam. She could slide into Sandra's place easily.

"Hi," Sam said with a shy smile.

Connor took another sip of his drink before turning to her. *Damn. She really was unbelievable. A little young, but what did that matter?* "You look lovely," he told her coolly, kissing her cheek. When he went in for it, he felt her stiffen and brace for a kiss on the mouth. He loved putting women off balance like that, plus the knowledge that they would let him do whatever he liked from the jump.

"Thanks," she said, tugging at her short dress and sliding onto the barstool next to him.

It was barely a slip of a dress, if you could even call it that. Black with a satin finish, it bared her toned shoulders and showcased her deep cleavage. Connor loosened his tie slightly as he broke out in a sweat. Eyes continued to be drawn to her from every corner of the room. It was exactly the reaction he wanted.

Let's see what Sandra and her family think about this, he thought. But he shook the thought away. *Why are you thinking about Sandra?* Besides, if his plan went as he hoped, Sandra and her family wouldn't find out about Sam for a long time, if ever. *You just need a bride, not this 'til death do you part bullshit.*

"What are you drinking?" he asked her.

"I don't know. What are you drinking?"

"Scotch, eighteen years. Would you like a taste?"

She wrinkled her nose. "Tanqueray martini, extra dry with a twist," she said.

He was impressed. "For a second there I thought you were going to order an appletini or some other horrific concoction."

She laughed. "I drink gin martinis because I can tolerate the taste just enough so that I sip it slowly. Fruity cocktails I'd just down like soda."

"And the lemon?" he asked. "Why lemon instead of olives? I thought women liked the olives in martinis. You can eat them sensually, like cherries in an Old Fashioned."

"Real martinis are served with lemon," she said simply.

He looked her up and down. *Maybe there was more to this girl than he'd given her credit for.* "Another for me," he told the bartender, "and a Tanqueray martini, extra dry with lemon, for my friend." She bristled at the word "friend," just as he'd expected.

"So, how was—" she began.

"I didn't ask you here for small talk," he interrupted. She looked surprised, but kept her mouth shut. "Look, I'm going to be really upfront and transparent with you. I have ulterior motives."

"Yes, so you said at my office," she said, and thanked the bartender for her drink.

"There's a lot more at stake here with my failed engagement than some kind of broken heart."

"Oh?" she asked. As she lifted her drink to her lips, he gently clinked glasses with her. "You have to maintain eye contact when you toast," she told him. "Otherwise, it's bad luck."

"My father is the CEO of Trezor Security," he said.

"That's where I know your name from!" she said. "I've been trying to figure it out."

"Yes, well. And I'm next in line for the illustrious throne, as he likes to call it. I've just signed on as Chief Operations Officer, but there's always been a catch built into these contracts. My father believes his eldest son is only cut out to take over once he's married."

"I see," she said. "So… that makes sense why you were so angry about the engagement. But, I mean, did you love her?"

"Sandra? Yes, I suppose so," he said. Connor mulled it over. *Had he loved Sandra?* He'd never given it much thought. "I thought she was… appropriate," he said.

"Appropriate," Sam repeated.

"Well, none of that matters now. What matters is why I asked you to meet me."

"You want me to help you get her back or something?" she asked.

"Hell no. What's the matter with you?" She looked surprised at his anger, and he forced himself to calm down. "What I mean is I'd like to ask you to play the role of my fiancée. Just for my father. You know, until things settle down and I'm secure in the COO position."

Sam was silent as she stared at the bar table. She put down her drink and licked her lips. "And what if I have a boyfriend?" she asked.

"You didn't mention anything about one when I asked if you were married or engaged. Wouldn't that have been the opportune time to bring up a love interest?"

"I guess so…"

"Let me be clear. I don't actually *want* you." He could tell that stung, but it put her back in her place. "You're cute and all, but if you have a boyfriend or whatever, that's fine. This isn't a physical relationship I'm asking for."

She smiled at him. "Then what's in it for me?"

"What's in it for you? How about this?" He grabbed a cocktail napkin and pencil from the barkeep's station and wrote down his offer.

When he slid it to her, her eyes widened. "Twenty-thousand dollars?" she whispered. "That's… that's…"

"Not enough? Make it twenty-five," he said.

She shook her head. "No way, that's insane. That's way too much."

"You don't think you're worth that much? I won't argue. What lower sum do you suggest?"

"No! I mean, this is crazy," she said. "It's just crazy."

"It seems I've piqued your interest, though. Couldn't you use a little extra money? You're young, what, twenty-three? Twenty-four? Surely there are student loans you want to pay off, vacations you'd like to take."

"I can't believe this," she said. He could tell she had started to warm up to the idea.

"I should stress, though, that the money is contingent on us actually getting married. Fully, legally married."

"Married?" she asked, her voice small.

"Well, at least engaged for a long time. You'd need to really sell the part. I'd need you at family affairs, but I would always give you plenty of notice for events. When you're not with me, your time is free to do with as you wish. I only ask that in your genuine romantic life, you keep everything discreet. The last thing I need is my father finding out you're banging some kid in the break room."

She blushed. "There's nobody," she said.

"So. Will you do it?"

Sam chewed her lip and looked once more at the slip of paper.

"I'll give you five thousand as a good faith effort as soon as you agree," he said. How much sweeter could this deal get for her?

"What if we try it out for a month? Just to, you know, make sure we get along okay. And I wouldn't take the five thousand until after the month is up."

He shrugs. "That's up to you. But if you want to pretend being my fiancée for a month for free, go for it."

"This is kind of exciting, actually," she said. "I feel like I'm some kind of heroine in a romantic comedy."

"Don't get too excited," he warned. "Your first job is tomorrow. There's a family dinner planned, and it'll be the perfect time to introduce you. I'll pick you up at six, and bring the paperwork and the ring."

"The ring?"

"Well, yes, I'd already told my family I got you a four-carat engagement ring from Tiffany's. Which, speaking of, I'll have to buy another tomorrow. Do you know your ring size?"

"Um, five and a half? I think."

"You'd better know."

"Five and a half."

"Good. Put your number in my phone," he instructed. When he handed her the iPhone, it wasn't a blank contact screen. It was editing the contact for Sandra Brewer.

"Sandra Brewer," she said.

"That's your name from now on. Though I think Sam is an okay nickname. Shouldn't cause much of a fuss if it slips now and then."

She plugged her number in. "Well, Sandra," he said as he slid his phone into his jacket pocket. "Thank you for meeting me. I'm looking forward to our business arrangement."

"I like a challenge," she said. She finished her cocktail and shook his hand. "So I'll see you tomorrow, my intended?"

"I hate that word," he said. "In fact, all words that have to do with being engaged are pompous."

"Well, you *are* my intended," she teased. "I'll see you tomorrow. Don't be late."

He watched her wind through the crowd, all eyes once again on her. Through that nothing of a dress, he could see every swerve of her ass. As she passed by a particularly attractive couple, the woman caught her boyfriend staring at Sam's tits and shoved him roughly in the chest.

Connor laughed to himself and looked down at his drink. Sam was going to be a handful, that's for sure. Maybe he shouldn't have been so impulsive with this plan—or with choosing her. *Should I have gone with someone just a touch less attractive?* he wondered.

3

———

SAM

Sam watched as a gleaming white Mercedes pulled into her driveway at six o'clock sharp. She was more nervous than if this had been a real date. *Snap out of it! This is just a job. A totally crazy job, but still a job.*

She watched Connor step out of the car in an impeccable bespoke suit. He was unnervingly handsome, but such an ass. *Well, look at him. I guess he's earned it.*

He carried an envelope in one hand and jogged up the steps of her little clapboard duplex. "Hey," she said, opening the door. "You're right on time."

Connor let his eyes graze over her, unflinching. "And you look presentable enough to meet my family, I suppose."

She blushed and bit her lip. If he only knew it had taken her two hours to pick her outfit. She'd finally gone with a slim-fitting, tailored business suit with a silky violet blouse underneath. The jacket flared out in a nearly peplum fashion.

"This is for you," he said, handing her the documents. "You can sign them later if you like, at the end of the month."

She took the documents, and suddenly the whole thing felt real. *Can I really do this?* she wondered. The money was good. Really good. But maybe she needed to consider the whole too good to be true warning here.

"And this," he said, pulling that telltale turquoise ring box out of his pocket. "Size five and a half."

Her mouth dropped open. In lieu of a traditional diamond, it was a massive sapphire with clusters of diamond accents. "It's…"

"It's on loan for now," he said. "I'll need it back at the end of the night. Now. Let's get going."

He held the door open for her, acting the part of the gentleman. *I guess we're both acting.*

All day long, she couldn't get over it. Sam couldn't believe he'd had the nerve to propose such an incredible ploy to her—and she was even more surprised that she'd said yes. She sneaked another look at him. He looked *good*, she had to admit. Every time she saw him, he looked better and better. *Why me?*

She couldn't help but stare at the ring on the way to dinner. It fit perfectly.

"It's like Princess Diana's," he told her. She blushed when she realized she'd been caught admiring it.

"It's gorgeous," she said.

"Sandra had demanded a so-called traditional diamond, even after I'd explained to her about the blood diamond industry, how De Beers made up the whole a diamond is forever thing, and all. But I realized when I was at Tiffany's I'd never described her ring to my family. I figured I'd choose a ring I actually thought was beautiful enough for the girl wearing it."

Sam flushed a deeper red. "So, uh, where are we going for dinner?"

"Pineapple and Pearls," he said, speeding up on the highway.

"Seriously?" She was shocked. Sam had been to the upscale venue with clients before, but that was to look at spaces—not for dinner herself. It had taken all her professional gumption to not look shocked at the price tag when she was with clients.

"You don't like it?" he asked.

She looked at him quizzically. Was he being serious or making fun of her?

"So, let me fill you in on the family," he said. "My mom is harmless. She might get emotional though, fair warning. Let's hope she took her Zoloft today. My brother, Sean, is a little shit. I guarantee you he'll drink too much at dinner and might hit on you. But basically he's harmless."

"Good to know," she said, nervously pushing at the ring with her thumb.

"And my dad is just a royal asshole. He's… well, you'll see. But I'm guessing he'll be directing it at me, not you. So don't worry too much."

"You sure know how to put a girl at ease," she said.

His phone buzzed. "Fuck," he said, glancing at it.

"What?"

"Change of plans. Dinner at my parents' place."

"What? Why?" The idea of such an intimate surrounding threw her.

"Honestly, my father was probably always planning this. He likes to throw a wrench in things and see how I react."

When they pulled up to the imposing house with the impeccable lawn, Sam could hardly believe it. A fleet of Audis were in the driveway. *You can do this. Put on your movie star charm,* she told herself.

"Ready?"

"There they are!" his mom called cheerily when he ushered Sam inside. "Sandra, sweetheart, it's so nice to finally meet you. Let me see that ring. Oh, it's gorgeous, Connor! But why not a diam —"

"Actually, it's Sam," Connor corrected his mother.

"Pardon me?"

"She goes by Sam."

"Oh, my mistake. Would you like some Prosecco, dear?"

"Yes, Mrs. Harris, thank you," Sam said, shining her megawatt smile at the plump older woman with perfectly coiffed silver hair.

"Not bad," Sean said, walking into the room with a beer in hand.

"Sam, this is my brother, Sean," Connor said as he shrugged out of his jacket.

"You got any sisters? Although I'm guessing any younger than you would be jailbait," Sean said as he eyed her.

"Don't you have a video game to play or something?" Connor asked as he waved Sean away.

"Where's your dad?" she whispered to him.

"He likes to make a grand entrance," Connor told her as he began to craft his scotch on the rocks at the bronze cocktail table.

"Come, dear," Mrs. Harris said. She handed Sam a flute of sparkling wine and took her elbow. "Dinner's about to be served, and Mr. Harris is dying to meet you."

Sam raised her brow at Connor and allowed his mother to steer her into the formal dining room. The focal point was the massive oak table with a buffet and china display lining the walls. Wainscoting met with gold-leaf wallpaper and the soaring ceiling was trimmed in intricate crown molding. Hanging above the table was a huge crystal chandelier.

From the gorgeous flower arrangements to the carefully displayed china and gilded flatware, it looked like something out of a fairy tale. "This is beautiful," she told Mrs. Harris. "A Christofle flatware set, incredible."

"You know your table settings," Mrs. Harris said, impressed. "Here, sit by me."

"I'm an event manager for luxury clients," Sam said. She waited until Mrs. Harris sat before following suit, and the woman smiled at her knowingly.

Connor took the seat on the other side of Sam.

"Good job with this one," Mrs. Harris told him as she nodded at Sam. "Beautiful *and* educated."

"So, we finally get to meet the famous fiancée." Mr. Harris burst into the room like a storm. Tall and foreboding with a balding head and thick mustache to make up for it, Sam was used to men like him. They were the type who pinched her ass in meetings and stared at her chest without reserve.

"Mr. Harris," she said as he walked toward her. She stood and offered her hand. "It's such a pleasure to meet you."

He grunted, but took her hand reluctantly. "Well, I can see how you caught my son's eye," he said as he traced her curves with his eyes. "Sit, sit. Don't stand on my behalf."

Sean sulked in late and made a racket as he scraped his chair against the hardwood. "Sean, *please,*" Mrs. Harris said.

"So, Sandra—"

"Sam," Mrs. Harris corrected.

"Oh, Sam now, is it?" he asked with a cocked brow. "Sam, tell me. What is it your parents do?"

"My parents?" she asked. "Well, uh, my father passed away—"

"Oh, I'm sorry to hear that," he said.

"Thank you, but it was a long time ago. My mother, she does a lot of volunteer work." Sam figured that sounded better than saying she was a grant writer for a small nonprofit. Connor smiled at her.

"That's good!" Mr. Harris said. "We have a strong philanthropy arm at Trezor ourselves. Any siblings?"

"Father!" Connor said as one of the servants set down plates with a single spoon of soup topped with caviar before Sam and his family.

"Just the amuse-bouche, dear," Mrs. Harris said to her. "Don't worry, we're not planning to starve you."

Mr. Harris swallowed the spoon in one bite. "And where did you go to university? Grad school?"

"Sam actually studied abroad, in a little private college outside Stratford-upon-Avon," Connor said. She looked at him curiously. *She had?*

"Doubt truth to be a liar, but never doubt I love," Mr. Harris said. "Shakespeare," he told the table. "But I'm guessing Sam already knew that. So, Sam. How long after the wedding do you suppose you'll be giving me a grandchild?"

She nearly spit out the hundred-dollar mouthful. From the corner of her eye, she saw Connor's jaw twitch in nervousness.

"Enough with the interrogations," Connor said. "Give her a little space." She felt his hand on her thigh and he squeezed. When she looked at him, questioning, he winked at her.

"Settle down, Connor, I have a right to ask these questions," Mr. Harris said. Sam narrowed her eyes and looked at him. She'd been around men like him all her life. Pushy, arrogant, thinking they owned the world and everyone in it.

"No, Sam doesn't have to answer such personal, assaulting questions," Connor said. He nodded to the servant to take his plate away. The tiny platters were replaced with salad dishes of chard, beets and goat cheese.

"Assaulting? I don't—"

"I'd like them sooner rather than later," Sam said sweetly, taking a sip of her Prosecco.

Connor looked surprised, but wrapped his arm around her shoulders. "Would you like a copy of her fertility planner?" he asked his father mockingly.

"Connor!" Sam said. She surprised even herself at her admonishment. "I apologize," she said to the Harris'. "Connor and I are just figuring out the timing right now. That's all."

"Back in my day we didn't need planners and timers to get our wives pregnant. Something wrong in the sack?" his father asked, looking from Sam to Connor.

"You know what? I think that's our cue to leave," Connor said. He stood up from the table and pulled Sam up with him.

"Oh, honey, don't go," his mom started.

Connor held up his hand. "I think we've had enough. Thanks for trying, Mom."

"I'm sorry about that. About the whole shitty lot of them," Connor said as he turned the ignition.

"It's alright! It's fine. It's not the first time I've dealt with a man like your father," she said.

Connor sighed as he backed onto the road. "Still, it could have gone much worse."

Really? It could have been worse than that? she thought.

"You know what? I think this is going to be a good fit for me. I do."

Sam sat quietly. She toyed with the ring and pulled it on and off her finger. *If was his idea of a successful dinner and a good fit, what was his idea of a failure?* Maybe this whole thing was too insane after all.

"I have certain expectations of my fiancée. It's outlined in the contract," he said as he drove her home. "The way you look, the way you behave, it's all critical. I'll let it slide that you raised your voice at me tonight —"

She frowned. "Did you have such expectations of your real fiancée?"

His brow furrowed. "Of course I did. And may I say, that while your outfit tonight might be good enough for work, it's definitely… *wanting*, if you know what I mean."

"What's wrong with it?" she asked, looking down.

"Appearances are everything in my world, Sam. You being hot isn't enough. Maybe that was my fault. I'll connect you with my personal shopper and tailor tomorrow."

She didn't say anything else. Connor seemed satisfied with the conversation. "Ring?" he asked as he pulled up to her house.

She slipped it off and handed it to him. Connor put it back in the box and tossed it in the glove compartment. "Well, thanks for—" she began.

"I'd love to stay and chat, but I have a date," he said.

"Oh! Of course. Well, bye."

"I'll be in touch," he said. He didn't drive off until she was inside.

What the hell was that? She wondered if she'd bit off more than she could chew.

4

CONNOR

He closed his new office door behind him and breathed in the scent of freshly-arrived mahogany. Connor couldn't lie to himself—the office of the Trezor COO was *sweet*. He fell into the hand-stitched leather executive chair, breathed in the rich scent, and spun it around. He felt like a kid at Christmas. Or at least what he figured normal kids felt like at Christmas. His holidays had usually been spent vacationing in Saint-Tropez while hired nannies watched him and Sean.

Everything his father did was top notch. It was one of his few good qualities. The new Trezor building, just erected four years ago, had been designed by a contemporary architect under the watchful eye of his father. The tallest building in the up-and-coming area, it featured nothing but black glass and industrial steel piping.

It was a monster, and now Connor was at the top of it. Peering down from the eighteenth story, Washington, DC, looked like a miniature of a town. *You can own this town if you play your cards right.*

The corner office was opposite his father's and offered stunning views. "Mr. Harris?" His newly assigned personal assistant poked his head in. James was dressed in a bright seersucker suit with brown and white Oxford shoes. "Your father asked me to go over today's itinerary with you."

Connor sighed. "Yeah, James, come on in." He was well aware of why his father had hand-selected a male assistant for him. His father didn't want any kind of office sex scandal marring the family name.

"It's a busy day!" James said, settling into the heavy wooden and leather chair across from Connor. "I've also synced your calendar with mine and scheduled pop-up reminders at forty-minute increments along with GPS instructions when applicable."

"You're certainly… efficient," Connor said.

"Thank you, sir," James said. "At eight o'clock, so in one hour, you have a meeting with *GQ Magazine.* At eleven there's a short meet and greet with *Forbes.* Then you have a lunch meeting at 1789 Restaurant with *Entrepreneur*—their veal sweetbreads are to die for if you haven't had them yet—then, at two—"

"Whoa, whoa, this is all today?" Connor asked. "And why *GQ*? This is all to discuss security business?"

"Well… not exactly," James said. "Your father thinks it's prudent to take advantage of your Navy experience, try and get some photo shoots going to make a big splash about your joining the company."

"SEALs," Connor corrected him.

"Excuse me?"

"I was a SEAL, not just in the Navy. And I'm the Chief Operations Officer, not a goddamned male model."

"Could have fooled me, sir," James said.

"Look, James, I'm guessing you have my entire life scheduled on my calendar for weeks out, right?"

"Everything that's been booked so far, sir, yes," he said. "Although I must say, your father is ordering new appointments nonstop, so I don't encourage you to consider your calendar set in stone by any means."

"Right," Connor said. "Can you just give me a few minutes? I'd like to look over my calendar in private if you don't mind."

"Certainly, sir. I'll be back in twenty minutes to escort you to your first appointment."

"I don't need—"

"Your father's orders, sir."

"Yes, of course."

James shut the door behind him and Connor fired up his tablet. The next six weeks were absolutely booked with meetings, lunch and dinner dates, and cocktail outings with the heads of magazines. *You're a goddamned figurehead of the company, not the COO. You don't have a single damn responsibility besides looking good in a suit.*

Connor groaned and rested his head in his hands. He pushed the old-school intercom button on the desk that connected instantly to James's Bluetooth. "James?" he asked. "With all these lunch and dinner engagements on here, what does that 'plus F' mean?"

"Those are the appointments in which your fiancée is expected to accompany you," James said.

"Seriously?"

"Seriously."

"You know, she has her own job—screw it, can you send this schedule to Sam for me?"

"Doing it now, sir."

"And while you're at it, talk to her yourself. She's going to need a new dress—scratch that, a new wardrobe for all this. Is that something you can help her with?"

"*Definitely,* sir," James said, the excitement evident in his voice.

Connor rolled his eyes, switched off the intercom and leaned back in his chair. *Does Sam have a family as crazy as this? Surely not as powerful, but maybe—just maybe—she has a hint of what it's like.*

Hell, he didn't even know if she had much of a family. He thought of her and her mom during the holidays, an empty seat intentionally left there in memory of her father. Maybe she had a hot best friend who was like a sister and spent Thanksgiving with her. Perhaps she had a gaggle of cousins who played the part, from the protective older brother to the sniveling little snot of a kid.

"I need to know more about her," he said out loud. He'd already made a royal mistake, making up where she'd gone to college on the fly. That was an easy fix, though.

He could always find out the truth and say she'd just studied abroad for a year. Surely his father wouldn't dig too deeply.

Connor looked at his schedule again. James would be prancing through the door in ten minutes. *Why wait to get to know the basics?*

He dialed Sam's number—or Sandra Brewer's as his phone indicated. "Hello?" she said. Her voice was groggy.

"It's past seven, why aren't you awake?"

"Who is this?" she asked sleepily.

"Your *fiancé*," he said.

"Oh!" she said, suddenly awake. "Sorry, I haven't saved your number in my phone yet."

"Yeah, well, you might want to get on that. Look, you've probably already got your schedule for the next few weeks from my assistant James. But I think it's best if we meet up before this mess of black tie affairs to get to know each other a little better. I'd rather get our stories straight rather than thinking up basic facts on the fly."

"I agree," she said. "That whole thing with you saying I went to school in the UK—"

"Sorry about that," he said. "I panicked. This whole thing, it's new to me."

"I'd hope so," she said. He ran through his head of possible places to meet her. Somewhere nice, upscale. Somewhere she might wear another one of those sexy little dresses. He felt himself start to harden thinking about that black dress from the night at the bar. Even the suit she wore to meet his family, with that feminine low-cut neckline had sparked his interest.

Not that he was *attracted* to her by any means. At least not beyond appreciating a sexy body when he saw it. But what was the harm in looking? After all, she was his fiancée.

"Oh my God! Connor? Did you see this? Do you know how many appointments I'm supposed to be at?" Clearly, James really was on top of everything.

"Of course I saw it," he snapped. "I scheduled them." She didn't have to know it was his father pushing for all of this.

"How am I supposed to make time for all of this? I'm not going to quit my job to play your arm candy, if that's what you have in mind—"

"Calm down, nobody asked you to quit your job, did they?" he asked. "If you'll actually look at the calendar instead of flipping out, you'll see they're all short lunch meetings and dinner engagements. Surely you have a lunch break, don't you? And you eat dinner, correct?"

"Well, yeah," she said.

"Good, then I don't see what the big deal is. Your office is close to downtown anyway. I'll pick you up and make sure you get back to work in a timely fashion. I'm sure the clients will understand that you're a career woman."

"A career woman?" she asked. "Really? What, did you step right out of a *Mad Men* episode?"

"You know what I mean," he growled.

"Mr. Harris?" James asked, sticking his head in again. He tapped his bare wrist and raised his brows. "*GQ,*" he mouthed.

"Alright, alright," Connor told him. "I'm coming."

"Sandra, we need to talk about this later. I'll text you the time and place to meet tonight and we'll talk about this in person. Consider this a day off from appointments. I'll explain to the clients that you had a conference all day today."

"It's *Sam,*" she said in exasperation.

"Yeah, yeah, you know what I meant," he said.

From the door, James tapped at his wrist with more insistence.

"I see you!" Connor said. He hung up on Sam without saying goodbye.

"You're just going to adore the E in C of *GQ,*" James gushed. "He's fantastic, really."

"E in C?"

"Editor in Chief," James said slowly. "The last time I met him, he was wearing the most delicious pair of Helmut Lang trousers, and I told him—"

"James, if you don't mind, can we keep the chattering to a minimum? It's not even eight o'clock and I already have a headache."

"Oh my! That's my fault. We'll swing by and I'll get you your coffee to enjoy on the way. Americano with a dash of cream, one sugar and a shot in the dark. Correct?"

"Yeah, how'd you—you know what, never mind. That's right."

James smiled at him. "I know how important the ritual morning cup of coffee is," he said. "Have you tried French press before? I personally find it to be quite…"

Connor sighed and let James babble on. By the time they pulled up in front of the building to meet with *GQ*, Connor was adept at tuning him out almost completely. In fact, James' voice was quiet soothing background noise. Either that, or the coffee was working its magic.

As they walked through the lobby and James led him toward the tucked-away café in the back, Connor's phone buzzed in his jacket. He pulled it out and there was a text from Sandra Brewer. *WTF does your assistant need to know my bra size for?*

He smiled to himself. James was nothing if not thorough, and probably oblivious of how intimate the question was. "Hey, James," he said.

"Yes, sir," James replied, eager to be of service.

"When you find out Sam's bra size, can you let me know? I uh, want to surprise her with something for the anniversary of the day we met."

"That's so sweet, sir! Of course I will. But wouldn't it be easy for you to just peek in her dresser?"

"You'd think so, wouldn't you?" he asked.

5

SAM

Sam shifted uncomfortably in her seat. The plush, velvet lining of the intimate booth at the Old Ebbitt Grill did nothing to soothe her nerves. The Victorian-era saloon was draped in swankiness. Even though the sun had barely set, already couples were tucked away in their own little worlds, making out. Single men in suits that cost more than her rent circled like birds of prey.

She'd gone over their brief phone calls and texts but couldn't figure out why he wanted to meet with her now. Sam had the schedule, she'd carved out the majority of her time for him to bullshit with his pompous clients. *What else could he want?*

All she'd received was a text with the time and place. *Thank God I looked up the place.* She'd been about to show up in her work clothes, but after she read the reviews she'd rushed home and changed into a slinky silk red dress. *I have to say, I fit in perfectly.*

Finally, she saw him sweep into the room and head straight to the bar. Somehow, Connor had a way of filling up a venue with his presence. Women's heads twirled to watch him—some of them pulled away from their boyfriends and husbands to do so.

She felt her heart hammer. When he turned and smiled at her, it went out of control. *He's ridiculously handsome. Way too handsome to be faking a marriage. It just doesn't make sense. Unless… maybe he's gay. Or dating somebody who's way taboo.*

Sam bit her lip and watched him maneuver through the crowd. One of the women's boyfriends got upset and tapped her shoulder to peel her eyes off of Connor.

"Hey," Connor said. "I thought you'd be at the bar." A waitress already rushed toward them. The same waitress Sam had watched for the past ten minutes in hopes that she'd come and refresh her drink.

"What can I get you?" the waitress asked, breathless. She couldn't take her eyes off him.

"Another champagne for my *wife*?" Connor asked as he looked at Sam's empty flute. He stressed "wife" with a touch of meanness.

She blushed at the word and nodded.

"Actually, why don't you make it a bottle for us to share. Perrier-Jouët Belle Epoque, if you have it."

"Oh, I'll check," the waitress said, crestfallen.

"I think you just broke her heart," Sam told him as the waitress left.

"I have a knack for that," he said.

She frowned. The sudden meeting, the bottle of champagne. *Was he planning on ending things before they really got started?* She knew she shouldn't have mouthed off so much this morning when he'd had that litany of requests.

"So, any brothers? Sisters?" Connor asked. She was surprised by the sudden interest.

"Um, a sister. Emma. But she's away at school."

"Does she look anything like you?" he asked. His eyes probed deep. "Sorry, never mind. Where did you really go to school?"

"Georgetown, local," she said with a shrug. "It helped save money on room and board."

"So you never did the whole sorority thing," he said with a nod. "Major?"

"Math education."

"Math? Then how the hell did you get into event planning?" he asked. The waitress arrived with the bottle and poured them both a glass. She stomped off without a word.

"Math education, it's different. It's, like, how to teach math," she said. Sam lifted the flute, held his eyes and toasted.

"The question still stands."

She shrugged. "I got burned out. Didn't want to get my master's in education right then, and you can't really do much in regards to teaching with just a bachelor's."

"So you're smart," he said.

She nearly spit out the champagne. "What?"

"I'm guessing you have to have some intelligence for that degree. That's surprising, you should lead with that more."

"Excuse me? Lead with that?"

"Exactly. When you meet quality men, I mean." He leaned back in the booth and surveyed her.

"If you're referring to yourself, you and I met when I was trying to smooth over my fumbling coworker," she said. "Apologies if I didn't teach you the Collatz conjecture while making sure a five-tiered fondant cake in the shape of a swan was invoiced to the right address."

"Eight," he said.

"What?"

"It was eight tiers. And it was hardly a swan."

She rolled her eyes. "Whatever."

"And you said Georgetown, so I'm guessing you grew up here."

"Great Falls," she told him.

"Really? That's... moderately affluent," he said.

"You seem surprised."

"It's just with not having a father —"

"I *had* a father," she said sharply. "And he didn't pass until I was in high school."

"Sorry," Connor said as he lowered his head.

The anger sloughed off of her. *It wasn't his fault that he could act like such a prick, really. Remember his family, or father? It's a miracle he wasn't a psychopath. Maybe he's just curious about you!* "It's okay," she said. "Sorry I snapped."

He smiled. "Who's your best friend?"

"I, um, I don't want to tell you that right now. If it's brought up at events, just say I'm too busy with work."

"A secret," he said as he leaned toward her. "But why?"

"I met her in college," Sam said slowly. She finished her second glass. "She was a history major." *Shut up.* "She's, um, the sister of the president."

"President of what? Which company?" Connor asked. He was inches away from her.

She raised her brows. "The *United States*," she said.

"Oh. What? You mean your best friend's —"

She hushed him. "Can we just move on?" she whispered. "How about you give me some information?"

"I think going to my parents' place was plenty of intel," he said.

"Okay, then what's up with the schedule from hell? Why am I required to go to all these lunches and everything?"

"Good question! You should ask my father. It's not my doing. I just showed up for my first day as COO this morning and was handed this schedule by the most annoying assistant ever."

"You mean James? He seemed nice. If a little nosy."

Connor groaned. "It turns out, I'm more the 'face of Trezor' than the COO. I don't know, this is something I'll have to address with my father. I don't want to talk about it anymore, I've spent all day dealing with it. All I can tell you is that I don't want to be on this ride any more than you do, but for now we're both stuck with it."

She felt sorry for him. He was willing to put on this big façade, pay her a generous amount to play along, and it turned out all his dad had done was slap a title on him before showing him around like a prize pony. "Connor, I'm sorry," she said. "That's terrible."

"Thanks," Connor said as he finished his own flute. "It certainly makes my father look good, though. So, back to you. How's the love life?"

She looked down and felt a cold sweat as it broke out along her skin. *What the hell was she supposed to tell him?* "Not very exciting at the moment," she said quietly.

"No? Why not, is there something wrong with you?" he asked.

She bristled at the accusation. "Wrong with me?" she asked. "Thanks for the vote of confidence. That's your wife you're talking about."

He laughed and held up his hands. "Sorry! It's just that you're hot. You're educated. You have a job. So, what's the deal?"

She chewed on her cheek and debated how much to tell him. Somehow, she didn't think he'd be very impressed if she said she'd only gone all the way once, when she was young—and that it was nearly traumatizing. "Just busy," she said with a shrug. "What are you, some mother from the 1950s trying to get me married off?"

"I just can't figure it out. That's all," Connor said. "So, you're not dating—"

"That's not what I said," she replied quickly, covering. "You asked about my love life. The guys I'm dating don't really qualify as much more than a little fun." She smiled at him as she regained her footing in this odd dance.

"Guys," he repeated. "As in plural."

She nodded. "I mostly prefer models," she said. *Well, at least that's true!* "Which makes the pickings kind of slim in DC. But you know how it is."

"Good on you!" he said. "I'm proud. Impressed."

She shrugged. "They don't ask many questions. They like to party, so it keeps things light." *Another tidbit of truth. You're really on a roll! Connor doesn't need to know that a lot of partying equates to not remembering what they did sexually... or not.* Sam had no idea how many models stumbled around the city, sure they'd had sex with her.

She noticed Connor's jaw twitch with that last comment, so she backed off and sipped some champagne. "Well, good," he said. "I'm seeing people, too." He sounded like a petulant child who'd realized he was losing his favorite game.

"I have no doubt," she said with a laugh.

He eyed her. "I'm hoping, of course, that with all your partying and philandering with models, you can still be a professional with this arrangement."

"Of course I can!" she said. *Shit. Was this all a trap?*

"I know I told you that when we're not together, your time is yours to do with as you wish," he said. "But honestly, that's when I thought you were largely a home-body. If I'd known you were going out all the time, dating a bunch of people who were in the spotlight—"

"They're *male* models, Connor. They hardly show up in PopSugar."

"PopSugar?"

She rolled her eyes. "It's like a celebrity site. Never mind. I'm just saying, you don't have to worry about me."

"I certainly hope not," he said. "I thought I was hiring a girl who could hold it together. And look good doing it."

She blushed and wished she could take back some of her bragging. Especially since it was far from reality. "You did. You are," she said.

"Excuse me for a moment, I'm going to get a club soda from the bar. Do you want one? Where the hell did the waitress go?"

She shook her head no and watched him as he made his way to the dark bar that shone so brightly it reflected the twinkling liquor bottles that lined the shelves. *God, he's so muscular. It's evident even through the suit.* Of course, given that the suit fit him perfectly, it was no surprise.

Connor turned quickly and caught her staring at him. He raised his shoulders in a gesture of annoyance as if asking her what she was doing.

Sam turned bright red and stood up. She grabbed her jacket and realized all that champagne had made its way into her head. *How could I be so irresponsible?* She needed to get out of there before he found out just how tipsy she was.

"I need to go," she told him as she sidled up next to him at the bar.

"Oh, okay. Do you need a ride, or—"

"I'm good," she said as she touched his arm. It was rock solid. "Thanks for the drinks."

She made a beeline for the door, desperate to get out before she got herself in trouble.

6

CONNOR

"It doesn't look good, us not arriving together," he told her again as he headed toward the Hay-Adams hotel.

"I'm sorry, but I told you I had a client meeting! Besides, what kind of gala starts at six o'clock?" she asked.

He could hear the stress in her voice and tried to relax for both of them. "It's okay," he said. "And, to answer your question, the kind of gala that's full of octogenarians hungry to open their pocketbooks for the right charity. This is like midnight to them."

"You're really selling this event," she told him.

He smiled. "By the way, you're wearing something James had delivered to you, right?"

She groaned. "Yes! And it seems ridiculously formal to be wearing when the sun's still up."

"It'll be fine. I'm pulling up to the valet now. Text me when you're almost here and I'll come down and meet you."

"Okay."

"And you need to be on tonight."

He'd only done one round of the room when her text came in. Connor was grateful for the excuse to do something. He'd already spied his father as he schmoozed with an ancient woman whose scalp shone through her white hair.

Sam was just taking the valet's hand to help her out of the car when he got to the bottom of the stairs. She was absolutely breathtaking, and James had earned his keep. She wore a perfectly tailored emerald green gown with beading at the hem that made her green eyes even more striking. It looked almost modest from the front, but when she turned he saw it was completely backless. Her nearly black hair swept into a chignon highlighted the olive skin of her toned back.

Sandra had been pretty, but she'd never quite looked the part—as much as Connor hated to admit that. Sam looked it and acted it. Immediately, she gave him a huge smile and her professional veil was draped all around her. He offered his elbow, and she'd barely taken it when they were bombarded with people.

"Is this the fiancée we've heard so much about?" Connor couldn't recall everyone's names, but it didn't matter.

"Yes, this is Sam," he said, and she turned into the ulti-mate socialite. Sam moved from group to group with ease. She passed out genuine compliments to the women, remembered details when they ran into them again hours later, and even managed to hold the men's attention without flirtations. Everyone was hooked.

Connor watched her work the crowd, impressed by how she always managed to shine while she still made sure he was at the center of it all. He'd known some women like this, which included his mom years ago in her prime. Only so much of it could be taught. Like grace, it was largely natural.

Whoever I end up with, however many years from now, will have to be elegant like Sam, he thought to himself as he watched her lightly touch the arm of a trustee and laugh.

"Champagne?" he asked her.

"Yes, honey, thank you," she said.

However, when he returned with the glass, she was alone for the first time that night. He handed her the flute, but she put it aside, disgusted. "What, no alcohol tonight?" he asked.

She turned red. "I'd rather not get myself into trouble, if that's okay," she said.

He was confused. *Since when did she not drink at all?* "Okay, if that's what you want. You'll need to at least have sparkling cider in a flute though. There are my parents," he said. "At five o'clock. Don't look."

"Connor, you're being ridiculous," she said.

She didn't even have a chance to turn around before his mom spotted them. From across the room, he saw his mom latch onto his dad's arm as she started to drag him toward them. "And, action," Connor whispered to Sam.

"Hello, sweetheart," his mom said. She pulled Sam to her and kissed both cheeks. "Don't you look lovely! This color really suits you. And Connor, of course, handsome as always."

"Thanks, mom," he said.

"Making good contacts?" his father asked gruffly. "I saw you with the Hoskings earlier. They seemed quite taken by your fiancée here," he said.

"Yes, I think the evening is quite successful," Connor said.

"And Sam, you're not drinking, I see," he said. "Just be careful, before the wedding and all."

"What do you mean by that?" Connor asked.

"Well, you're obviously trying to conceive. Which is fantastic, but we don't need any gossiping about a shotgun wedding—"

"What the hell is your problem?" Connor growled at his father, who looked around the vicinity and raised his brows in a warning.

"It's okay," she said. "Your father's right. Don't worry, sir. I'm just detoxing and cleansing my body for now. Children aren't in the plan until after the wedding."

Connor's mouth ached from gritting his teeth, and his father somehow continued to egg him on without saying a word.

"Hey," Sam said. She touched his shoulder lightly, just enough to distract him. "How about the cider you promised me?" When he looked at her, he couldn't help but notice the swell of her breasts beneath that tight satin gown. Sam followed his gaze and turned a bright red. Her embarrassment sobered him up instantly.

"Right," he said. "Why don't you accompany me? Mom, Father, we're off to mingle more," he said. Connor took her hand and led her away.

"Do you mind if we step outside a moment?" he asked. "I could use some fresh air."

She shrugged. "It's your dime."

"I want to apologize for that," he said.

"You don't have to apologize for anything. Honestly, your dad's not that out there, you know? I've experienced worse."

"I meant I wanted to apologize for my behavior," he said cautiously.

"What do you mean?"

"I just—I don't know. Being around my parents, it just enrages me somehow. They're the only people who can unnerve me like that. I feel like I'm this perpetually angsty teenager around them. I can't shake it."

"That's normal," she said gently. "Only our parents can drive us crazy like that. Well, and love. Or so I've heard."

"I just want you to know, that I understand you're a paid contractor. If the tables were reversed… I don't know. I wouldn't like being put in that kind of situation."

She sighed. "It's not exactly the most normal job I've ever had. And honestly, getting this personal with the people in your life, it's not as easy as I thought it would be."

"It won't happen again," he promised. "I guarantee it. I want you to be as comfortable as possible, and if that means exerting more control over my family, that's what will happen."

"Okay," she said with a sigh. "I mean, it's not like I have any context to compare this gig with. Let's see how it goes."

"Great," he said. *She was a trooper, that's for sure.* "As a good faith effort on my part, would you mind escorting me to my car for a moment?"

She cocked her head and looked at him curiously. "What do you have in mind?"

He took her hand and headed to the employee elevator. "Sit for a moment," he said as they reached his car, opening the passenger door for her.

Flipping open the console, he pulled out his copy of the contract and scribbled an amendment. *Should the CLIENT take advantage of CONTRACTOR at any time post-May 20, 2017, "advantage" defined by CONTRACTOR'S terms, CONTRACTOR will receive a $10,000 bonus in addition to the $25,000 agreed upon project rate, and will be immediately released from the contract and all duties herein.*

"Well? What do you think?" he asked, showing her the amendment.

"I think you should have been a doctor with that handwriting," she said. "Look, Connor, I didn't ask for any of this. I think you're blowing it way out of proportion."

Maybe she was right, but he couldn't get over that look of shame she'd had when she'd caught him staring at her chest. "I know you didn't ask for it," he said. "But I'm a man of my word, and I've always taken pride in ensuring my employees and contractors are well cared for. It'll just make me feel better knowing you're protected."

She flushed, and a smile played at her lips. "Okay," she said. "If that's what you want."

"Do you want to sign it now?" he asked. "I can have James deliver it to my attorneys first thing in the morning."

"Now?" she asked. "The whole thing?"

"Unless you have doubts about the arrangement still, which I understand. I know we said we'd give it a month —"

"Now is fine," she said, and reached for the pen. "I think we're pretty much in this whole thing by now. What's the point in waiting?" She signed her name in pretty, flowing lines.

"Awesome," he said.

She laughed. "Awesome? Maybe you are a teenage boy at heart."

"You should be so lucky. But we should get back to the party now. Who knows how many crypt keepers are just dying to fawn all over you and try to wheedle information about Trezor out of me."

She rolled her eyes. "They're not so bad," she said. "Besides, by now everyone's probably so drunk we can talk about last week's *Saturday Night Live* skits and they'd swear it was the most intellectual conversation ever."

"You're lucky," he said.

"Why's that?"

"You're not completely jaded by being surrounded by these people yet. You can still find something interesting about them."

"Well, that's my job," she said with a smile.

"And apparently, you're going to work for every penny," he said. "Come on. I owe you a sparkling cider, I believe. You know, just in case you get knocked up sometime soon and plan to embarrass my father with a shotgun wedding."

She groaned. "You can't blame the poor man for hoping."

"I wouldn't if he actually wanted grandchildren for normal reasons. He's just desperate to make sure his royal reign continues. You should talk to him! I'm sure you can negotiate a bonus if you make a male grandchild happen within a year of the wedding for him."

She gave him a funny look. "Now that would be a miracle," she said. "Kids weren't written into that contract of yours." She poked him in the arm, but he had a feeling she was only half kidding.

"I wasn't being serious," he said.

She turned and got out of the car. Connor paused, unable to take his eyes off her ass. The material hugged the round curves perfectly, and the back plunged so dangerously low he could see the two dimples above her cheeks. They nearly begged him to press his thumbs into them.

He shook his head and got out of the car. *No more of this crap. You're playing with fire.*

7

____

SAM

She spent all day Saturday recovering from Friday's gala—which ended up going until the wee hours of the morning. *Damn Connor for suggesting these old people couldn't party.* They were raging drunk by midnight, and Connor couldn't manage to get them out of there until past two in the morning.

Sam was sure a day of laying low on Saturday would give her enough energy for Sunday's luncheon. However, when she woke up Sunday morning, she still needed two espressos to get going.

Connor texted her at ten o'clock. *Pick you up at 11:30,* he said. She groaned and headed into the shower. Her feet were pissed at her. She couldn't remember the last time she'd worn stilettos, standing, for so many hours straight. Normally, at a club or a work event, she felt like she had permission to go barefoot at a certain point. Or slip into the foldable ballet flats she used to pack in her purse. But with Connor, she didn't even have to ask to know that would be a violation of her contract.

She let the hot water soak into her skin and soothe her muscles. Sam worked through what she saw had become a daily ritual now. Complete hair removal, exfoliation, deep conditioning treatments for her hair, and an immediate post-shower moisturizing regimen.

Sam padded into her bedroom to flip to the James-approved outfit of the day. He'd even gone so far as to attach notes to each outfit specifying the date, time and occasion of her dresses.

She pulled it out and found another little backless number. He sure liked those, and was probably totally unaware of how awkward it was to wear little stick-on cutlets over her breasts instead of a real bra. This dress was floral, bright, and flared out at the hips before stopping at her knees. He'd paired them with a strappy pair of silver Jimmy Choos.

Connor came to her door, and she thought she saw him look her up and down, but it was impossible to really tell behind his reflective sunglasses. "You look nice," he said.

"So, all James' note said was 'investors meet and greet.' Care to tell me more about my duties here?" she asked as Connor drove them to The Mansion on O Street. *I have to admit, I'm getting a serious introduction into some great venues and catering for work with all these outings,* she thought to herself.

"I'll basically be conducting information mini-interviews with some contacts. There will also be some investors, and potential investors, for Trezor there," he said.

"So my job is…"

"Arm candy," he said. "Sorry, babe. I have a feeling not too many WAGs will be there."

"Babe? WAGs?" she asked. "You're a strange one, you know that?"

"And just so you know, people won't be drinking. Well, drinking as much, I should say. For some reason people think it's okay to go bottoms up for hours when it's called a mimosa."

"Why are you telling me this?"

"Because it's also a smaller, more intimate gathering. Which means more eyes will be on us. We really need to sell the whole happy engaged couple shtick," he said.

"Got it."

Pulling up to the mansion, the valets had to have been sweating in their heavy velvet costumes. Still, they plastered smiles on their faces and rushed to open Sam's door. *We're all playing our part,* she thought.

Connor placed his hand on her back to guide her up the stairs, and she stiffened at his touch on her bare skin. He hadn't touched her so intimately on Friday night, mostly offering an elbow or taking her hand. Something about this made her feel like he knew her too well.

"That's the Steins, over there," he murmured under his breath. He took a mimosa for himself, but she shook her head when he offered her one. Without a word, he got a flute of just orange juice for her. "They're current investors, but have lowered their funding in recent years. His wife is big in philanthropy. Shocker. Here we go."

She warmly greeted the wife first, followed by the stodgy husband. Sam had found that older women weren't intimidated by her, and there was rarely any cattiness in their interactions. It was a welcome change from the twenty- and thirtysomethings she was used to dealing with at the office.

"Connor, you have such a lovely fiancée," Mrs. Stein said. "And so eloquent, too. Not many young women have both qualities these days, I'm afraid."

"I count myself very lucky," he told her, before he disappeared with her husband to talk business in the corner.

"I must say, we thought Connor would never get married," Mrs. Stein said. "He had a bit of a… reputation. As I'm sure you know. But, alas, men never change. All it takes is one good woman to snap them out of that playboy state."

She smiled amicably at the older woman. "I do love a challenge," she said.

Mrs. Stein laughed, her blue-tinted hair swishing around her face. "Don't we all, dear."

Connor returned, his big smile matched with Mr. Stein's. The older man patted Connor on the shoulder. "You have quite the shark of a future husband," he told Sam. "I can't recall the last time someone squeezed such an impressive percentage out of me."

Mrs. Stein rolled her eyes. "Probably the last time you were four drinks deep before noon, love," she said.

Connor excused them, and his hand returned to the small of her back. Sam blushed once again, unable to keep the flush out of her cheeks. But she couldn't help it. *Well, what do you expect? It's not like you've had much time to yourself lately, what with work being so hectic. You've had no time to relax. Or release any of that tension.*

She blushed deeper at the thought of getting herself off. Sam couldn't remember the last time she'd masturbated, or made use of that little silver vibrator Emma had given her for Christmas. The thought of dildos terrified her, which Emma knew. That's why the little bullet had been so perfect.

"You okay?" Connor whispered in her ear. She felt his thumb dip slightly lower down her back. It played at the waist of her dress.

"Yeah," she said, and smiled up at him. A twinge between her legs intensified when she was reminded of how handsome he was. *You better take care of yourself before you see him again,* she thought. *It's not his fault he's ridiculously gorgeous.*

Besides, he'd made his feelings perfectly clear when he'd signed those papers. *Who cares if he was checking you out before? If he even was!* He wouldn't be the first man to assess her and then pass her up. *Men are visual creatures, that's all.*

Sam ate just the right amount at the luncheon. Enough to ward off any talks of her being too uptight to enjoy herself. However, it would be hard to overindulge at a so-called luncheon where the only food was walking appetizers. She could hardly fill up on the occasional bacon-wrapped date stuffed with goat cheese that happened to mosey by. For the most part, she depended on glasses of orange juice.

"This thing is about wrapped up," Connor told her two hours after they arrived.

She nodded. "I think you've talked shop with just about everyone here."

"You running out of compliments to give the old women?" he asked with a smile.

"Hardly," she said. "I still have the one where I ask about their secret to such a youthful, glowing neck tucked away."

"Shark liver oil," he said.

"Excuse me?"

"They use shark liver oil. It used to be a main ingredient in Preparation H in America, but now they have to import it from Canada. It smells disgusting, but apparently works."

"Are you bullshitting me? How do you know this?"

He looked at her, surprised. "I thought everyone knew that. Isn't that what your male model boy toys use to keep that perpetual glow of a prepubescent?"

"You're so weird," she said.

"You like it. Hey, are you hungry? Do you want to grab a meal somewhere that serves more than a bite at a time?"

"Ugh, yes, please. The only edible thing here were those dates."

"You can't blame the elderly. I think your taste buds disappear or something after a certain age."

"Where are we going?" she asked as he lowered the top of the Mercedes and she wrapped her hair in a scarf.

"It's a surprise," he said with a wink.

"What is this place?" she asked as they rolled up to a simple, two-story red brick joint near Lincoln Park.

"You've never been to Kenny's?" he asked, incredulous. "It's the best barbeque in DC!"

The scent of the Southern-style BBQ permeated the air and made her mouth water. Connor ordered for them — brisket and ribs, collard greens, coleslaw and cornbread. "This is amazing," she said as they sat on the patio with their cafeteria-style plastic trays. Finally, she felt comfortable enough to slide out of her heels.

"I'm happy to be the one to introduce you," he said.

She licked the hickory sauce off her fingers and looked at him. *Maybe there's more to him than I thought.* "Tell me something," she said.

"What's that?"

"Anything. About you. I'd like to get to know my husband better."

"Not much to tell," he said. "You know I was a SEAL pretty much all of my adult life. I did a number of tours, saw the world — or, I should say, the parts most people don't really want to see. I was engaged to Sandra for my last deployment, we broke up, what, three weeks ago now."

"Three weeks?" she asked, shocked. "That's it?"

"Well, I figured you knew that. Considering we met because I went to your office to get the financial mess of it fixed."

"I know, but… I don't know, I didn't know you came to my work right after your engagement ended," she said.

He shrugged. "Why let tasks wait?"

"So why did it end? If you don't mind me asking." Sam had heard some of the details at the office, but wanted to know if there was more to the story than what Connor had said before.

He sighed. "It's not a very unique story. I thought we were happy enough. I went by her place to surprise her and take her out for lunch, and caught her on her knees with some guy's cock in her mouth."

Sam put down the cornbread slathered in butter. "Are you serious?"

"Afraid so," he said. "And the thing is? She didn't seem particularly embarrassed or anything. In fact, she tried to turn it around on me. Said that I just wanted some little military housewife or something."

Sam was shocked. *He was cheated on?* She couldn't fathom it. He could have anyone he wanted. "Wow," she said. "I mean… I guess I get now why you wanted to do the fake engagement."

Connor cleaned his hands with a wet wipe and leaned back. "So. Why are you doing the fake engagement?

What are you going to use the money for, if I can be so bold as to inquire?"

She blushed and reached for the first lie she could muster. "Down payment on a house," she said.

"That's really mature," he said, and looked at her thoughtfully.

Sam turned redder and dug back into the cornbread. She'd never even thought of owning property.

8

CONNOR

New Rihanna pulsed through the sound system at Kabin Lounge. The girl grinding into his crotch grabbed his hands and placed them dangerously low on her hips. She was hot with her hair styled into perfect beach waves and wicked coffin nails, microbladed brows and eyelash extensions—but for some reason he wasn't feeling her. Connor couldn't put his finger on it.

"I'm going for a drink," he shouted into her ear.

"Bay Breeze!" she said.

"Right," he said as he exited the dance floor. *There's no way in hell I'm getting this girl a drink.*

Connor leaned against the wall by the bar as he waited for the bartender to slide over a scotch on the rocks. His eyes were drawn to the entrance, and he saw Sam enter, flanked by what was clearly a model on one side and a hot couple on the other.

He squinted into the flashing pink lights. Sam was dressed in a white bandage dress that clung desperately tight to her. It glowed in the club's lights. The couple was made up of a man who was obvious military stock, though he had at least a decade on Connor. The girl had lush, thick red hair to her waist. Although the redhead seemed to be into the scene, the guy she was with had that telltale expression of boredom most men adopted in clubs when they were over the age of thirty. About ten feet behind them, two men in dark suits with clipped haircuts entered.

Connor took his drink, tipped the bartender exorbitantly, and moved farther into the shadows to watch Sam and her crew. *Maybe she wasn't bullshitting about the model thing after all.*

Sam placed her hand on the model's shoulder, threw back her head and laughed. However, when the model touched her waist and reached for her ass, she smoothly stepped away. The couple they'd come with had disappeared, and it was just Sam and her model.

Her date stepped up right against her and buried his head in her hair. She bit her lip and nodded, but when he went to put his arm around her she moved away. *What's her deal?*

Finally, he watched Sam say something to the model as she made her way—alone—to the bar. Connor walked briskly to the other end to cut her off and take her by surprise. He walked up behind her. "What would your husband think if he knew you were here?" he asked in her ear.

She jumped and turned around, her eyes big. "Connor!" she said and slapped him. "You scared me."

"That was the point. Drink?" he asked.

"Whatever you're having," she said.

"Expanding your palate," he said, "I like it." He gestured to the same bartender for another. "So, who's your date?"

"You certainly get right to the point, don't you?" she asked.

"I have a right to know who my wife is fraternizing with, I think," he said as he handed her the drink.

She rolled her eyes. "He's harmless. Mostly. Besides," she said as she brought the drink to her lips and took a generous swallow, "look." She pointed to the dance floor, where the model was already dancing with another girl. The same girl Connor had abandoned on the dance floor.

"I know that girl," Connor said. "Her name's Bay Breeze."

"Is that her stripper name?" Sam asked.

He just shrugged. "And who's the couple you came in here with?"

"What, have you been watching me?" she asked. The DJ segued into a Wale song, with Justin Bieber singing the hook.

"I keep an eye on my surroundings," he said. "You can't forget military training so easily."

"You should talk to Henry about that," she said.

"Is that your date? Kind of an old-fashioned name, don't you think?"

"*No*," she said. "My 'date's' name is Pierre."

"Figures," he said as he rolled his eyes.

"Stop that. Henry is the other guy that came with us. He's Ellie's, my best friend's, boyfriend."

"Wait, Ellie's the one who—"

"Yeah, yeah," she said. "Did you see a couple of guys in suits come in? That's her security."

"I saw them," he said. "They seemed out of place. But then again, so does the Henry guy."

"Henry's not much into the club scene, but he does it to appease Ellie."

"So, what, Henry's military, too?"

"SEAL, like you," she said.

"Don't know him."

"I think he got out before your time. So," she said, "who are you here with? Alone, on the prowl for some strange?"

"I love it when my wife talks dirty," he said. "Actually, no, I came here with some friends."

"Prove it," she said.

"What?"

"Prove it!"

He thought about it, even though her challenge was so transparent. *What the hell. If they were going to fake an engagement, shouldn't she know his friends?* "Alright," he said. "They're at the other end of the bar. But they're not in on any of this," he said. "So only meet them if you're ready to sell the whole engagement thing."

"Okay, okay," she said. "I feel like I'm dressed kind of slutty to be doing this though."

"You're wearing virgin white," he said. "What could be more wholesome than that?"

He took her empty hand and began to forge a path through the crowd. Huddled at the end of the bar was his small, but usual crew. His three buds from high school, two of them with their short-term girlfriends. Connor couldn't be bothered to learn their names, they moved through them so quickly.

"Hey, guys," he shouted over the music. "This is Sam. My girlfriend."

One of his friends didn't even bother to stop his mouth from dropping open. "Girlfriend? But didn't you just—"

"Didn't I just what?" he asked quickly.

"Nothing, man. Hey, Sam. I'm Chase, and this is Jay and Dan. We've known Connor forever, so feel free to ask us for any embarrassing stories about him. And this is my girlfriend, Anna, and Eve over there."

"Hi," Sam said smoothly to each of them. She worked her usual magic with ease. Connor was aware of the girls as they sized her up, on edge because of the clear competition. However, Sam had a way of putting snark to bed and lavished compliments on them.

"I have to say," Chase said. "You're, uh, not what I expected."

"No? What did you expect?" she asked.

Chase downed the last of his drink. "To be honest, Connor's type is usually blonde and dumb as a brick."

"Chase!" his girlfriend said, and smacked him on the chest.

"What! It's a compliment," he said. "I mean, I don't know you, Sam, but I can tell you're a smart girl."

"Since when is my type dumb and blonde?" Connor asked, honestly confused. Sandra hadn't been blonde. *Was that really what his friends thought of him?* He knew Chase could be an ass at times, but he was also brutally honest when he was drunk. And he was plenty drunk now.

"Uh, since THOT was all up on your junk," Chase said. He pointed to the girl who hanged off the male model. "Don't worry," he said to Sam. "Connor walked right away from that trainwreck."

"He can dance with whomever he wants to," Sam said with a smile. "It's who he comes home to that I care about."

Amidst whoops and hollers, Connor put an arm around her, and felt her stiffen. "You got yourself a good one for once," Jay said.

"Yeah," Eve slurred. "You should kiss her!"

Somehow, the little group rallied their thoughts enough to start a chant of, "Kiss her!" over and over. "C'mon, man, we're doing you a favor," Dan said.

Unable to think of a way out of it, Connor leaned down to meet Sam's lips. *Why not? She should be expecting this anyway. It's not like I'm asking her to sleep with me.*

He meant it to just be a peck, but as soon as their lips met he couldn't pull away. Her lips, though he knew they'd be soft and supple, were also magnetic. She tasted like just the faintest trace of scotch and her own sweet, natural self. Sam responded, and parted her lips.

She turned to face him, and he slid his hand from her shoulder to the back of her head. He traced her jaw with his thumb and pressed himself against her. He felt one of her hands on his back, and her breasts squeezed against him. Connor couldn't help it. He grew hard against her stomach.

Sam pulled back, startled and wide-eyed. His friends hollered some more, but simultaneously turned back to the bar as they realized their drinks needed refreshing.

"Sam!" The redhead, Ellie, was suddenly by their side. "We couldn't find you. We looked and—who's this?" she asked, and turned to Connor. Her big doe eyes searched his.

"Um, this is Connor," she said. Sam dabbed at her lips. "My, uh, my boyfriend."

"Your *boyfriend*?" Ellie asked. "Then who the hell was the guy you came—"

"Just a friend," Sam said.

"He didn't act like just a friend," Ellie said suspiciously as Henry approached from behind.

"He's gay," Sam said.

"Oh. Well, nice to meet you, Connor," she said. "This is my boyfriend, Henry."

"I've heard a lot about you," Connor said to him. It was rare to meet a man in civilian life that matched his height and brawn.

"We haven't heard a thing about you," Ellie said. He saw Henry nudge her.

"Sam likes her privacy," Connor said.

"Thanks for the tip. I've only known her for five years," Ellie said.

"As fun as this is," Sam interrupted, "I think I'm about to head out. I have a massive headache."

"Justin Bieber will do that to you," Henry said, clearly happy for the excuse to leave. "Ready?" he asked Ellie. Ellie looked out to the crowd with a pout.

"I guess. If my boyfriend and best friend are leaving, it would be pretty awkward for me to stay."

Sam gave Connor a look, said her goodbyes to his friends, and left with Ellie and Henry in tow.

"Damn, Connor, how'd you pull that?" Chase asked as soon as she was out of earshot.

"What, you think she's out of my league?" Connor asked. He took another sip of his scotch.

"Uh, yeah," Chase said as Anna rolled her eyes.

"She seems nice, Connor," Anna said. "Good for you."

"So are you hitting that, like, on the regular?" Dan asked.

"Oh my God! Could you be any hornier?" Eve asked. "Do you want, like, a play by play or something?"

"More like a blow by blow, if he can be bothered. Everyone here is getting laid besides me. Cut me a little slack!"

Connor remained quiet as his friends continued to talk about how much they liked Sam. "So, hey," Anna said as she slipped between him and Chase. "What was up with you on the dance floor with that girl, then? I mean, I'm guessing you and Sam are a new thing, but still—"

"Why don't you worry about your own relationship?" he asked and nodded toward Chase.

"Asshole," she said, and moved away from him.

9

SAM

"You promise?" she asked him as she drove her little hatchback toward Connor's second family home.

"My father will be on his best behavior, trust me," he said.

She smiled as she hung up and pulled off the highway — this was deep in the Virginia countryside. His father didn't really bother her, but it was a bit cute watching Connor squirm about him. And this time, it would hardly be her in a fishbowl setting. When Connor told her it was a "big political fundraising shindig," she could only imagine how big it would be.

Sam followed her GPS as it led her to a sprawling plantation-style home. The long driveway was lined with blossoming dogwoods, the white pillars of the sprawling home an homage to the estate's history. She drew in her breath as a hired valet rushed to her. *How much money did these people have?*

It was barely five in the afternoon, and already people were everywhere, champagne and martini glasses in hand. She passed by a lake stocked with swans and lily pads. In the distance, she made out a white horse stable and tennis court. A tipsy older woman laughed and crashed into Sam. "I'm so sorry, dear," she said. Sam smiled at her, happy that the woman's glass was empty.

Spread across the property and spilling out of the house, everyone was dressed to the nines. It was like *The Great Gatsby* had shot through time and arrived squarely in front of her. Another woman traipsed in front of her, wearing a fur shawl, the Virginia spring be damned. *Who wears fur still?*

Sam skirted the house and found the rear entrance. The original Dutch door opened onto a screened-in patio where one of what she could only assume were many bars stood. Finally, she spotted Connor surrounded by a group of young, beautiful women. They were clearly taken, and all smiled up at him.

A twinge of jealousy pulled at her. *What's your problem? You don't have any rights to him.*

Connor saw her and immediately broke away from the group of girls. "You look great," he told her.

She bit her lip and looked down. When she'd first pulled the short, fringed black dress out of its garment bag, she'd thought James had gone mad. However, she was so thankful for the relatively low, thicker heels with Mary Jane straps she hadn't asked questions. Now she knew James had known exactly what he was doing. The dress paired perfectly with the vibe of the event, and the shoes were ideal for walks around an estate. "Thanks," she said. Her eyes roamed back to the girls.

"Young, pretty things to make my father look good," Connor explained. "They might as well see the good stock first, right?" he smirked.

"And, what, then your father so they can see what to expect in thirty years?" She snapped her mouth shut, and knew she'd gone too far.

Clouds moved across his eyes. "Ouch," he said. "Let's get some champagne, shall we? For me at least."

"I'll have one," she said.

"Really?" he asked in surprise.

"In a water glass. Make it look like cider."

"You've caught on beautifully," he said.

He got their drinks, took her arm and directed her toward his father, who was circled by a small group. She drew in her breath to prepare for whatever miserable conversation she was about to endure.

"Then the boy says, I've only been a white kid for five minutes and I already hate you black people!" His father had just finished what she could only imagine was the most racist joke possible when they arrived.

Half of the crowd laughed politely, while one young man simply widened his eyes.

"Connor, there you are!" his father said. "And my grand-child-making machine. Isn't she lovely? Won't take a sip of alcohol, keeping that system clean as a whistle. Can you believe it?"

"Lovely to meet you," one of the women said to Sam, offering her hand. "What a gorgeous dress."

"I've told them to hold off until after the wedding," his father continued. "But," he said, as he breathed deeply, "with this fresh country air and romantic estate, I can hardly blame them if we have to bump the wedding date up a bit, if you know what I mean. Look at this girl! Legs like a thoroughbred. I tell you, I can't even imagine how beautiful those grandkids will be."

Sam couldn't help but turn bright red. She stared at her feet. Could she actually hate this man? Was that too harsh?

"Great to see you again," Connor said to the man next to him. He ignored his father's comments entirely. *Was he used to this? What happened to him coming to her rescue?*

"Excuse me a moment," she said. "Ladies' room." Instead, she went to the bar and ordered another champagne in a water glass. "When I ask for the cider, this is what you give me," she told the bartender as she tipped him a ten.

"Yes, ma'am."

Slightly buzzed, his father's comments lost some of their sting. She made her way back to the group, but couldn't help but stare at Connor as she did. Even if he could be a bit arrogant and pompous at times, hadn't he earned it? *Look at him!* Every woman there, no matter who they were, lusted after him. *Me included,* she admitted to herself.

As she finished half her glass, she came up behind him and wound her arm through his. Connor was in the middle of entertaining two middle-aged women who looked at him like they were starved.

"So, this is the lucky girl," one of the women said, her voice dripping with envy. "To be young again," she said.

"Connor!" his father called. "Come here a moment and meet Mr. Lee. Sam, you don't mind."

She wanted to ask if that was a question or a statement, but kept her mouth shut. Suddenly, the secret champagne really did rush through her and she started to hunt for the restroom as Connor was engulfed in more small talk. She found one without a line upstairs, but the door was locked.

When it opened, out tumbled one of the most stunning girls she'd ever seen. Her platinum blonde hair was pinned up in a tight chignon, offsetting her gray eyes and perfect cat eyeliner. Behind her was her friend, in Havana twists with the most striking eyes Sam had ever seen.

"Hey! Hey, you're the fiancée, right?" the blonde said, clearly drunk. Her friend dabbed at her nose.

"Connor's fiancée?" she asked. "Yes, I am. I'm Sam," she said, and smiled warmly at the girl.

"Oh my God! Then you know!" she said.

"Know what?" She really had to go to the bathroom, but the two girls blocked the doorway.

"You know… like, how big he is!" she said with a laugh.

"Shut up!" her friend said. "Don't be rude."

"I'm not, I'm congratulating her!" she said. The blonde leaned into Sam and put her arm around her. "Really though, like a friggin' horse! Am I right?"

"Um. Yeehaw?" Sam said. This was the exact conversation she didn't want to be having.

"No, though. I mean it's been a few years since I was with him. Not since you, of course! But I give you mad props, girl, for snagging him. The first time we were together, I couldn't walk right for like a week."

"Jesus," her friend said. "Can we go now? Sorry," she said to Sam.

"Um, thank you," Sam said to the blonde. The two girls stumbled down the hall.

Are they for real? she wondered as she closed the bathroom door. *Could he really be that big? I mean, she's assuming we've slept together so there's no point in exaggerating, right?*

She looked at herself in the antique mirror. "Get it together," she told herself. Sam pulled her red MAC lipstick out of her purse and reapplied it. She pressed tissue between her lips and blotted her face next. "You can do this."

When she exited the bathroom, an older man waited there. "Sorry," she murmured.

"Not at all," he said, his eyed glued to her cleavage. "It was well worth the wait."

She hurried downstairs and started to look for Connor again. As always, he'd found himself in the middle of a cluster of women. These were younger, perhaps still in high school. She raised her eyebrows at him, and he shrugged. "This is my fiancée, Sam," he told them. One of them audibly groaned. "These are the, uh, daughters of some of my father's colleagues."

"Oh, then I'm sure you all have a lot in common," Sam said sweetly as Connor put his arm around her waist.

"You're really pretty," one of the girls offered.

"Thank you. So are you," she said. "I love your shoes." The group of girls giggled and wandered away. "You mind staying out of jail, sweetheart?" she asked.

"Hey, they came up to me —"

"That's what they all say." She teased him, but her eyes kept wandering down to his crotch. *Was the blonde being serious?* "I met one of your exes in the bathroom," she said.

"I cringe to imagine which one," he said as he directed her toward a group of retirees.

"Blonde, which I know is your thing of course," she said.

"You'd have to be more specific. There's a lot of blondes here."

"A lot of blondes you've slept with?" she asked.

He shrugged, and her eyes roved once again to his package. She couldn't tell much, what with the suit jacket.

"She was beautiful," she admitted. "I think her friend was snorting blow in the bathroom."

"I know who you mean," he said. "And she's hardly an ex. We hooked up a couple of times, she's the granddaughter of one of my father's investors."

"She only had nice things to say about you," Sam said.

"Well, there's a surprise. Good evening," he said to the group as he plastered on his business smile. "Have you met my fiancée, Sam?"

She got back into her groove with small talk. Still, she lost track of some of the details because she couldn't stop checking out what the blonde had promised her. *How big is big, though? I mean, isn't it all relative?*

"...don't you think, dear?" the woman standing in front of her asked.

"Yes, ma'am," she said. Sam had no idea what she was agreeing to.

"I do, too. You know, most young people these days..."

The woman continued to blather on, and Sam stared again at Connor's midsection. *Is there such a thing as too big? I imagine you'd have to work up to it...*

Her eyes moved upward and took in his wide chest. How masculine his hands were that held that scotch tumbler. When she reached his face, she realized he'd been staring at her the entire time. Connor nodded at her and gave her that smirk that she'd seen him dish out to every girl that fawned over him.

Embarrassed, she immersed herself in the boring conversation with the woman.

"...the Tories, *that's* who we need to be emulating," the woman said.

"I couldn't agree more."

10

CONNOR

onnor gestured for the waitress and settled back into his white chair at Barmini. It was an eclectic gathering, and not what he'd planned—a small group of investors, his closest friends, and Sam. However, it had worked out beautifully.

Chase and Jay were completely taken by Sam. He glanced over at the trio, who were buried in deep conversation. Sam was dressed in a smart white suit with a deep neckline and sky-high stilettos. James had matched her to the décor, yet she managed to outshine even the swankiest of cocktail lounges in the city.

Chase laughed loudly and Jay couldn't tear his eyes away from her. *Can't say that I blame them.*

"For real?" Jay asked Sam. "Damn, how'd you get seats like that?"

"I'm an alum," she said as she sipped at her scotch with just a splash of soda. "Any time you guys want to go to a game, just let me know."

"Awesome, man," Jay said with a fist bump to Chase.

"I don't know why you put up with this guy," Chase told her, and nodded toward Connor with a smile. "He can be a pretty demanding SOB, right?"

"Oh, he's not so bad," Sam said. She smiled across the table at Connor warmly.

Connor knew he should work the table, enchant the investors, but she commanded everyone's attention. Even the investors, save for one who clearly had tastes that differed wildly, weren't being very covert with their looks in her direction.

"Sam," one of the investors said to her. He didn't give a damn that he'd interrupted the conversation. "Tell me, what do you do?"

"Oh, I'm an event coordinator at an agency in the city," she said. "We manage pretty much every type of event, but this time of year it's mostly weddings. And the occasional over the top graduation party."

"Event management," the investor said. He stared at her with clear desire. "I can see how you'd do well at that."

She laughed and tossed her hair over her shoulder. "I have to admit, I thought it would be quite different when I started. But you haven't seen the wild side of people until their big event is on the line."

"I can imagine," the investor said. "Is this your first job post-college? I'm guessing you majored in communication or business, then. Very fitting for marrying Connor, here."

She shook her head lightly. "Actually, no, I majored in math education."

"Math?" the investor asked. She'd genuinely confused him.

"Math education, it's a little different," she said.

"Connor, you've got a smart one here," the investor told him.

"I'm becoming more aware of that by the day," Connor said as he took her in. There was something about her. Something that just reeled him in closer every day.

Sam wasn't just hot. She was truly beautiful. It was an intoxicating combination he wasn't used to. *Why did it take you so long to notice she was more than just another hot piece of ass?*

"Are you okay?" one of the investors asked Connor. It was the oldest man at the table, and one who stared nonstop at Sam's breasts. *Or at least, nonstop until he'd decided to call me out just now.*

"Yeah, fine," he said. He readjusted his position again in an attempt to hide the fact his dick was hard. *Thank God we're sitting down.* Every time Sam smiled, there was another awkward shift in his trousers. It was ridiculous, this power she seemed to have over his body. He knew he had to cut himself off after this drink. Not only did he need his head in the game for the rest of the night, but he couldn't promise he wouldn't hit on her with just a drop more of liquid courage.

Sam caught his eye across the table and looked at him funny. She raised a brow, and asked silently why he kept shifting around. He wrinkled his nose at her, and she giggled. That giggle was enough to turn his erection hard as steel. It took all his willpower not to groan in frustration—or go somewhere and jerk off just to get her off his mind.

"These stools are a bit uncomfortable," the one investor who had no interest in Sam said.

"The price you pay for minimalism and overpriced watered down drinks," he said.

"Oh, definitely," said the investor. "No lounge could get away with such nonsense a few years ago. But the hipsters persist. Yes, they do," he said. "White on white in a room full of people guaranteed to spill their drinks. What were they thinking?"

Eventually, the investors trickled out of the bar. The sun was setting, and Connor could finally relax. It was just the four of them, and it seemed so natural. Like Sam had always been a part of his crew, of his life. "So, shall we?" Chase asked.

Connor looked around the bar, which was packed already for a Thursday evening. "Yeah, this place is dead anyway."

"You gotta update your pop culture references, man," Jay said.

"Come on, it was a good movie!" Connor said. As they stood, Connor was grateful for the dim lighting and dark suits. *You need to stop looking at her at least for a little while. Otherwise, the whole bar is going to know you're hard for her.*

Chase clapped him on the back. "You bagged a good one, buddy," he whispered into Connor's ear.

He didn't know what to say. *It's all a sham.* The lies just piled on top of each other. First it was his family, now his friends. He'd thought it would be easy, this whole façade, but he wasn't sure how he felt about the whole thing. Part of him wished he could just start over. *What would it have been like if I'd dated Sam for real? Knock it off, you can't be thinking about things like that or 'what ifs.'*

Yet Connor felt a twinge every time he looked at her. It was a pull that was more than sexual desire—that he could have brushed off. At least until the show was over.

The four of them walked out of the bar together into the deep pink and purple light of the sunset. As they parted ways, both Chase and Jay pulled her in for hugs and kisses on the cheek. "Next time bring your girlfriends," she told them. "I could do with a little more estrogen at these things."

"Will do," Chase said.

"Can't," said Jay. "Single again."

"Ladies beware," Sam said with a smile.

"Nobody you can hook me up with? A sister perhaps?" Jay said with a smile.

"My sister's too young for you," she replied.

"As long as she's eighteen, ain't no such thing," he said.

Chase groaned. "Come on, I'm driving your drunk, inappropriate ass home."

"My friends really like you," Connor told her as they stood on the sidewalk and watched the guys head to their car. Small groups of women in cocktail dresses, men in suits, and couples who clung too tight to each other continued to pour from their daily lives into the bar.

She smiled up at him. "They have good taste, just like you," she said with a wink.

It was strange, how Sam seemed to have it all. Looks, personality, intelligence, charm and wit. She was the perfect girl. "I don't know," he said. "They never seemed to really like my ex."

Sam cocked her head. "Maybe that's why she's your ex, then."

He laughed. "Maybe you're right. Although, in Sandra's defense, they weren't around her much. I guess that's not much of a defense. We were together for years and she met them maybe five times."

"It was fun hanging out with them. Outside a club setting, I mean. It was… I don't know. A chance to get to see there's more to you than meets the eye."

He snorted. The vulnerability put him on edge. "Plenty of women would kill to get with what meets the eye."

Sam blushed and looked away. "You know what I mean," she said. "And, besides, wow. Way to go full cocky on me."

"I do know what you mean," he said softly. "Sorry." Connor looked at her and wondered. It was early, and she looked incredible. Underneath that fitted white jacket was just a slip of a silk camisole. *Should I invite her to the underground fight club I'm headed to? Or… shit, no. It's stupid to let her get so close.*

Sam started walking toward the parking lot, a few steps ahead of him. From behind, he couldn't stop himself from staring at her hourglass body. *Screw it, I've been trying for the past two hours not to indulge.*

She positively glowed in the fading light of day. From her shapely calves to the swell of her hips and that unbelievably small, tucked-in waist, she was sheer perfection. That short skirt showed off nearly every inch of those long legs, and *damn*, it killed him. Her curtain of nearly black hair cascaded down her back, a contrast to the white ensemble.

Maybe it's not so stupid to bring her. I mean, after all, it would really amp me up to have her in my corner, right?

Connor debated the pros and cons as they reached his car. The last time he was at this club, he really got waled on. He'd thought he could hold his own—he was a goddamned Navy SEAL—but when those boys fought like dogs, like their lives truly depended on it, it was another story.

He couldn't blame the guys, either. That money must seem like a lot to some of them. *What's the worst that could happen? She sees me get pounded?*

Actually, now that he thought of it, it didn't really matter if the guys at the club tore him apart or not. Whether he won or lost, it would surely turn her on. *Right? Women love that shit.*

"Hey Sam, do you want to go somewhere with me?"

She frowned. "Really, Connor? This was the last thing on my schedule today—"

"No, not for business. I mean for pleasure."

She paused with her hand on the door. "What do you mean?" she asked cautiously.

"Get in," he said, and gestured to his car. He started the engine. "If you really want to see another side of me, come to this club with me."

"Club? Connor, I'm really not in the mood for dancing and sloppy cocktails."

"It's not that kind of club."

"Not that kind of club? I am *not* going to a sex club with you, if that's what you have in mi—"

"No, no, nothing like that," he said. "You'll see when you get there. But you've got to trust me. Trust me?" He looked at her and could see the curiosity in her eyes.

"Well… okay," she said. "Am I dressed okay for it?" she asked, and looked down at her suit.

"Trust me, nobody's going to be looking at how you're dressed." He grinned, gunned the engine, and headed toward Washington Highlands.

11

SAM

She was nervous when they parked in what looked like an abandoned, decrepit parking lot with barbed wire fencing. But no way in hell was she going to let it show. Sam already felt way overdressed, and slipped out of the white jacket, pulled the silky cami out of her skirt and made do with a makeshift minidress ensemble.

"I told you, nobody's going to be looking at your outfit," Connor told her as he opened her door. She shrugged it off, but took his hand.

The party was in an undisclosed warehouse, the only hint of nightlife the occasional blare of music that sounded when the doorman let groups in or out.

"What you want?" the doorman asked, an imposing man the color of midnight. He barely glanced at Sam.

Connor leaned into the man and whispered something to him, which opened the gates to the roar inside. "Was that a *Fight Club* quote?" she asked him. Sam had to hurry in her heels to keep up.

"Maybe it was," Connor said. As they walked through a thick mess of curtains at the end of the hall, the click of her heels still echoed in the steel chamber, but below them and all around them were throngs of people. Kanye's "Black Skinhead" blasted through the speakers.

Sam was nervous as hell.

"Come on," Connor shouted into her ear. "Let's get you a drink." It was barely dark outside, and yet the people were slick with sweat. Molly-infused mayhem surrounded her.

As she waited by the bar behind Connor, she ran over the conservations she'd had with Chase and Jay. Connor had been wrong when he'd said his friends hadn't cared for his ex much. They absolutely loathed her. Of course, the guys had been drunk, but didn't that make them more honest—albeit a bit abrupt?

"Nobody was surprised she cheated," Chase had told her, his voice slurred. "We were just surprised it took him so long to catch her red-handed. Excuse me, black-handed."

"Chase, that's racist," Jay had said.

"How's it racist? It's true!"

Sam had simply smiled and shook her head while tactfully changing the subject. However, they both kept mentioning the ex over and over. *Why do you care? Be professional, and don't fall into any of these traps laying around.*

"So, what is this, some kind of warehouse party thing where everyone's high on E?" she shouted to him as he handed her an angry red cocktail.

"In part," he said.

"What's the other part?" she yelled at him.

"I'll show you." He took her hand, held it tight against his back, and started to lead her away from the massive dance area. In the back, behind steel doors which required yet another flurry of secret codes, there was no music. There was no dancing. There was just a cage topped with razor wire.

"What the hell is this?" she asked, and stopped abruptly. "Connor, if this is some kind of sick dog fighting thing —"

"Dog fighting?" he asked, incredulous. "Don't be ridiculous. You think I'd be into that?"

"Then what is it?"

"Underground MMA."

She breathed a slight sigh of relief, but was still on edge. She'd heard about these kinds of things, but didn't think they really existed. Or that she'd know someone who was into it. "So, are you betting?" she asked.

"Liam!" Connor yelled, and motioned to a short, muscular guy in a worn-out Everlast t-shirt.

Liam grinned when he saw Connor, gave him a nod, and continued to the abandoned DJ booth. "Alright you sick fucks, it's on in twenty. See Bernard to place your wagers."

"It's your new besties," Connor told her before she could say anything, and nodded to the door. Chase and Jay made their way inside. "Guys, watch out for Sam, alright? And you stick close to them," he told her.

"What are you—"

But Connor was already gone, disappeared into the darkness. "So, you come here often?" Jay teased her.

"All the time," she said, distracted. "What's he doing?"

"He'll be back in a minute," Chase said.

"So, is this where you pick up girls?" she asked. Sam tried to make light of the situation, but she was nervous and felt out of place.

"Let's get a drink," Jay said, and ushered the three of them to the quiet bar in the back. She looked down at her hand and realized she'd already downed the one Connor had given her.

"I know it seems weird, but a lot of military guys come here to blow off steam," Chase said. "They dance with some hot girl. They fight. You know."

She didn't know, but she also didn't want to act put off.

"You know the rules of MMA?"

She shook her head, and Chase gave her a quick rundown. "That sounds insane," she said.

He laughed. "That's the point."

"Here we go," Jay said. She turned, and the ring was lit up with blinding spotlights.

Liam was back in the booth. "Wagers are officially closed. Connor and Zohaib in the cage. Guys, we went over the rules backstage. Let's keep it clean. Or, hell, you know what I mean."

Sam's mouth dropped open. She would have recognized Connor anywhere, but he'd shed his suit in favor of boxing shorts cinched at the waist and nothing but wraps on his hands and feet.

She couldn't help but drink him all in. The chiseled stomach and pecs, the flawless muscles bunched up his arms and shoulders. That delicious V-shape that flew wildly down his torso. There was something animalistic in all of this that turned her on instantly.

Sam looked at the other guy, who seemed to be well matched in size and muscle to Connor. She worried her bottom lip, unsure of what to think. "Don't worry," Jay said into her ear. "Connor will be fine."

A bell rang from somewhere that seemed far away, and Connor and his opponent were instantly at each other. She put her drink down and covered her eyes when Connor took a hit squarely to the jaw, but quickly peeked between her fingers. Connor had the guy against the cage, which rattled rapidly. Connor punched him viciously in the stomach.

Blood was splattered across both their faces and chests. Connor's white shorts were flecked in bright red. Relatively, it was fast—ten minutes at most. But it was way too long for Sam.

They were suddenly surrounded by people who pushed and cheered. The entirety of the dance floor must have been crammed into the back room. Every time a blow was landed, especially on Connor, she cringed.

He pinned down his opponent and went at him with unreal swiftness. Finally, the opponent tapped the cage floor. "It's over," Chase told her. She let out a long breath, unaware that she'd been holding it.

Liam was holding up Connor's fist, which was covered in blood. Chase and Jay went nuts beside her, whooping Connor's name, but she couldn't find the strength to do more than lower her hands away from her face. Connor and his opponent hugged briefly and patted each other's back as they exited.

Connor bounded out of the cage and jogged over to them. She noticed every girl he passed followed him lustfully with her eyes.

"Good work, man," Chase said, and pounded Connor's back.

"Wasn't nothing," Connor said, his breath already returned to normal.

Sam looked at him, inches away. Covered in a sheen of sweat and patches of already-dried blood, she saw another side of him. A rawer side, the one few people knew. As they made eye contact, she licked her lips, thirsty.

Connor's gaze moved to her lips. The kiss was inevitable. But when she tasted him, the salty, coppery blend, it turned her on even more. When his tongue flicked against hers, she felt wetness start to spread between her legs and let out a moan into his mouth.

She felt his hand on her waist as he pulled her close. His other hand was in her hair, and he pulled tight.

Jay cleared his throat and laughed awkwardly. "You guys want to get a room?" he asked.

Sam broke away from the embrace, flushed and her breath heavy. She knew she should be embarrassed, apologize to Jay, but she just couldn't stop herself. Connor looked so intense up there, and during the fight, in her deepest thoughts, all she'd wanted was to be the focus of that intensity. *Is that normal?*

Someone called Connor's name in the distance and he looked away from her. The spell was broken. *What in God's name are you thinking?*

It wasn't that big of a deal to kiss him in front of his friends. Besides, they'd kissed before, at that club. *But that was different. And it didn't feel like this.*

Still, it was to be expected that they kiss in public. Otherwise, how were they going to sell this whole thing? *Stop making excuses and rationalizing it to yourself. You know you didn't kiss him as part of your job.*

A blonde who barely fit into her dress sidled up next to Connor. "Oh my God, you were amazing! Amazing!" she said.

He laughed. "Thanks, Tiffany," he said, and gave her a pat on the shoulder.

Sam stiffened and picked up her drink. *Right. You have good reason to steer clear of him. Not only did his friends spend two hours talking smack about his ex to you, but you swore you'd stay professional—to him and yourself.*

The blonde gushed all over him, and she had to admit Connor gave some effort to ward off her affections. But he didn't introduce her to Sam. Instead, he tried to hand her off to Jay. "Have you met my buddy, Jay?" he asked Tiffany. "Ex-SEAL, too. I'm sure you'll see him in there next."

Tiffany glanced at Jay and considered. She was easy to read. But Tiffany had eyes only for Connor, that was evident.

Sam slipped away while Jay ogled Tiffany and Chase went back to the bar for another drink. Connor didn't even see her go. She looked back once, and saw the blonde feel up Connor's muscles.

She was already halfway home in an Uber when he texted her. *Where are you?*

Sam considered not replying, but knew that was childish. *Omw home. Tired, had to go*, she replied. She wanted, so badly, to say something snarky about him letting the blonde flirt with him, but stopped herself.

Ok. You mad? I just kissed you because of the fight, u know. Adrenaline gets me going, can't help it.

It's okay, she replied. *Probably good for the show*, she added.

I would've kissed anyone, he replied. *You just happened to be there.*

She slammed the phone onto the seat. *You're such a fucking fool*, she thought.

"You alright back there?" the Uber driver asked, a young girl probably in college.

"Yeah. Just so you know, men suck. And they continue to suck way after college."

"That's why I'm gay," the driver said.

"Oh."

"I'm just kidding. I mean, about the reason *why* I'm gay. But trust me, women are just as batshit crazy."

"So there's no hope then," Sam said as the car pulled into her driveway.

CONNOR

"James, it's been thirty minutes. You're telling me you can't find my father?" he asked him.

James shifted nervously in front of Connor's desk. "I'm sorry, sir. I've been trying—"

"Nobody's paying you to try, James," Connor said. "Screw this, I'll just go find him myself."

"But, sir, you need to prep for the afternoon meeting. And I have some documents that need signing—"

"Who's in charge here? You, or me?" Connor asked. He looked down at James' hand on his arm.

James gulped and slowly removed his hand. "You, sir. As you wish."

Connor was frustrated. The one time he actually needed to get hold of his father for a pressing business matter, and the bastard was nowhere to be found. He walked swiftly around the floor to his father's wing and burst into the reception area.

"Oh! Connor, your father is indisposed —" His father's receptionist stood up and waved at him.

"Is he, now?" Connor asked, and rushed to his father's closed office door.

Connor flung the door open, only to find Sandra spread-eagle on his father's desk with her skirt hitched up to her navel. Her tits hung out of her blouse while his father pounded into her, his trousers at his ankles.

"Connor!" she gasped, and rushed to cover her breasts.

His father turned slowly, as his fat and saggy ass jiggled below his button-up shirt. "I thought your mother taught you to knock," he said.

"What," Connor began coldly, "the fuck is going on here?"

"I—I came looking for you," Sandra said as she pushed herself away from his father and pulled her skirt down. "This isn't what it looks like, I swear."

"It's not what it looks like?" Connor said quietly. "It's not what it looks like?" He could hear his voice start to raise, but he couldn't stop it. His father's receptionist shut the door behind him.

"It's not! I swear," she said. "I—I came here with a proposal for you." She started to cry, but her bullshit didn't work on him anymore. "I'm sorry! I want you back. I came to ask for you back. And then —"

"I figured you were too busy with your magazine shoots or whatever," his father said. He pulled up his trousers and lit a cigar. "So I took her up on the offer. One of us may as well benefit."

"You piece of shit," Connor said. His fists were clenched, knuckles white.

"You know what I don't get, though?" his father asked with raised brows. "This girl here, she says her name is Sandy. Seems you have a thing for girls with similar names. Is that just a coincidence, I can assume?"

Connor's mind reeled. Sandra pulled at his arm, mascara streamed down her face. *Be careful, be careful what you say.*

"I used to want to be like you," he told his father. "Or, at least, be as rich as you. But you're disgusting, you know that? You filthy fuck."

"Don't you dare talk to me that way, boy, you understand?" His father made a move for him, surprisingly fast, like one of those bulls in Central America that gets a hot pepper stuck up its ass during a rodeo.

Connor lunged away from his father instinctively, putting the massive oak desk between them.

"Stop it!" Sandra screamed from the corner of the room. Connor glanced at her and saw one of her breasts still hung out of her shirt.

"You shut the fuck up, you useless bitch," his father told her. From the opposite end of the desk, he eyed Connor. "That the best pussy you could pull? It was subpar at best," he said. "Maybe that new one of yours is better. In fact, I'm sure she is. I'll have to sample it for myself."

"Fucking asshole," Connor said, and he raced around the desk at his father—who didn't move or even flinch.

"What are you going to do?" his father asked. A mean smile unfurled from below that waxed mustache. "Hit me? Try it. See what happens. See if I don't cut you off in a second."

Connor breathed heavily, but some practical part of him must have been listening. "What about Mom…"

"Your mother? Your mother knows all about it!" his father said. "Boy, you really are thicker than I thought. But if you want to make her more miserable, give her all the gory details, be my guest."

Connor growled, shocked at the raw noise that erupted from his throat.

"You listen to me. And listen good. If you step out of line, in any way, you're done. You hear me?"

"Go fuck yourself," Connor said. He turned on his heel and started toward the door. Sandra, still sobbing, started to hobble after him.

"Think about all you have to lose," his father said, his voice almost lyrical. Connor stopped, but didn't turn around. "Your trust fund. Your job. Your inheritance. Sean might be a drunk, but I'll leave it all to him in a minute if you cross me."

"You wouldn't," Connor said softly.

His father laughed. "You want to bet on that? And if you're thinking you can make it on your own, I won't stop there. I can make sure you can't get a job higher than mall security if you screw with me. Not here, not anywhere. Hell, I can even stop you from reenlisting if I'm so inclined."

Connor's breath was shallow.

"Of course, I might not do that," his father said. "No. I might just let you run right back into the Navy. And you can die in that hellhole overseas for all I care."

Connor didn't respond, but opened the door calmly. He could feel the wary gaze of the receptionist as she watched him, worried that he was about to do something rash.

"Connor," Sandra said as she followed him down the hall. Out of the corner of his eye, he watched her button up her shirt and do her best to walk in just one shoe. "I'm sorry, I'm sorry."

"You make a scene in front of the office, and I'll slit your goddamned throat," he hissed at her. She snapped her mouth shut, but continued to follow him. He didn't dare tell her to leave, lest it cause a scene.

James was open-mouthed as he watched Sandra trail Connor into his office. "Should I bring some tea—" he began, but Connor held up his hand to him.

Sandra shut the door behind her. "I'm sorry—"

"You've said that already. Quite a bit," he said. "What the fuck are you doing here, Sandra? And what the fuck were you doing with my father?" He balled up his fists again and paced back and forth in front of his desk.

"It was all so confusing," she said with a sniffle. "He told me—he told me you were engaged. *Already.* I didn't believe him, so he showed me some pictures… who is she?"

"You have no right to ask me that," he said, and looked at her sharply.

"You're right. Sorry. But he… he told me that you'd already moved on. And so, I figured I'd lost you for good. I was… I was going to leave, then he propositioned me with—"

"With what? Are you a whore now? A real, bona fide prostitute?"

"No!" she said. Fresh tears appeared at her eyes. "But he just… I mean, it was a lot of money."

"How much?"

"What?"

"I'd like to know how much my ex-fiancée is going for on today's market."

"It doesn't matter."

"Yes, it does."

She bore her toe into the plush white carpet. "Three thousand."

"Three thousand dollars. You fucked my father for three thousand dollars."

"Well, not really—"

"What do you mean?"

"I mean, you kind of walked in on us before he gave me the money. So, really, *you* owe me —"

"Fuck off, Sandra," he said, and shook his head in disbelief.

"You're such an asshole!" she yelled.

James popped his head inside. "Everything okay, sir? Do I need to call someone?"

"Call someone?" Sandra screamed, and turned on James. "Yes! You can call the goddamned HR department to cut me a check —"

"Call security if you don't see her walk out of here within ninety seconds," Connor told him.

"Yes, sir," James said, and clicked the door shut.

She turned to Connor, utter confusion clouded across her face. "How could you?" she asked. "I'm your fiancée. We were supposed to get married in a few weeks. You act like you never loved me at all."

"No, that's you," Connor said. "Leave, Sandra. And don't ever contact me again. Trust me, it's in your best interest."

"I won't —"

"Would you rather security carry you out?"

She looked him up and down, and tried to decide if he was serious. "Fine," she said.

Sandra turned, as poised as she could manage with one shoe, sex hair and a mascara-stained face, and marched out.

Connor sighed. *Why did you do that? You hate this goddamned job anyway, you should have just walked out of here for good.*

"That was a crazy one," James said. He carried a pot of chamomile tea on a silver tray.

"You're telling me," he said. "Thanks."

It was a miserable job, mostly, but there were certainly benefits. *Just play it cool, just a little while longer. Don't let him get to you!*

"James. Did you know? Did you know what my father was doing?" he asked, and looked at James' back.

James turned slowly. "I knew he was doing unspeakable things to a young woman in his office," he said. "I didn't know you knew her."

"I don't just know her," Connor said. "She's my ex-fiancée."

"Yes, I—I gathered that from what she just said in your office."

"Oh. You heard that, huh?" he asked, suddenly embarrassed.

"I'm afraid—your father's office is soundproof. Yours is not."

"So… how many people heard?"

"I can't be certain, sir," he said. "Probably not a lot. It's nearly the lunch hour—"

"Thank you," he said. "You can go."

James shut the door, and he buried his head in his hands. *Let this be a reminder. You can't trust a single damn female, especially around your father. No exceptions. But what about Sam?*

He groaned as he thought about it, and especially at the threat his father had made about her. *But she wasn't like that. There was no way Sam would do him dirty like that. Would she?*

His leg shook as he weighed the information in his head. He thought he could trust her, for the most part. What he knew about her. Then again, she was getting paid to play the part of his fiancée. *Fuck. What am I supposed to do?*

He couldn't exactly keep Sam away from family functions. That would look suspicious as hell. But he also couldn't trust his father around her, and he didn't know how much he could trust her. If Sandra would screw his dad for three thousand, what was Sam's price?

13

────────

SAM

Sam could hardly believe it. A Saturday completely free from any engagements—from Connor or work. Ellie had called that morning, but she'd let it go to voicemail. The second time Ellie had called, she'd placed her phone on airplane mode. *To hell with it, treat yourself, you deserve it,* she'd thought.

She woke up late, went for a leisurely morning run, then ran the hottest water she could stand for a long soak with a bath bomb. She sighed as she sank deeper into the water. *This is what I need more of.* The water stung her feet. No matter how many pedicures she got, and by now it was on a weekly basis, those constant stilettos James loved to get her tore her apart.

Wrapped in a fluffy white towel, her hair tied in a topknot, Sam fell onto her bed and let out a moan. It wasn't even noon yet, and the morning light streamed through her gauzy curtains. *I wonder what Connor's doing?*

She let her fingers move to the edge of the towel and inch up her thighs. Gently, she circled her clit. The thin strip of hair she let remain below was still wet from the bath. Sam bit her lip and thought of how Connor had looked that night at the underground club. How he'd tasted. How wet he'd made her with just a kiss, and of course before he'd been a total ass to her.

Sam unwrapped the towel and let the sun wash over her naked body. With her knees pointed toward the ceiling, she slid a finger into her mouth and took it back to herself. As she flicked across her clit, her nipples hardened. She kneaded her breasts with her other hand.

She slid her finger into her folds, surprised by how wet she was already. But when she thought about Connor's body, about that hardness she'd felt pressed against her that night in the club, she couldn't help herself. Sam let out a moan, coated her finger in her own juices, and circled her clit harder, wildly. "Connor," she gasped out. She pinched her nipples harder, and her back arched.

She was close, deliciously so. Eyes closed and legs spread wide, she imagined him on top of her. His scruff would rake across her cheek as his lips moved from hers to her neck. She imagined his length sliding slow and controlled into her, his muscled stomach pushing hard against her clit with every thrust. When his mouth reached her breasts, it would take her right to the edge.

The doorbell rang. *Goddammit, Ellie.* She worked herself faster, turned on by the thought of having a time limit. "Fuck me faster," she'd tell Connor. "Someone's coming."

It rang again, insistently. "Sam, I know you're in there! Your car's in the drive."

She froze. *Fuck, it was Connor.* She was so close to coming it hurt, but there was no way she could finish with him just a few feet away.

"I know it's your day off, but I need to talk to you," he called. "Why's your phone turned off?"

Frustrated, she let out a mewl and grabbed her short, red robe from the back of the chair. "Coming!" she called, and nearly laughed at how appropriate that response was.

Sam hustled to the door, her damp hair hung in long ropes down her back.

"What?" she asked as she answered the door. *Damn, he was good looking.* If she wasn't already about to orgasm anyway, she would have been as soon as she'd opened the door. She bit her lip and looked at his jersey shirt pressed against his chest with sweat.

"Oh, sorry, I didn't know you were in the shower," he said. She couldn't read anything in his eyes because of the sunglasses. "I was just on a run, and was in your neighborhood, so…"

"So?" she asked, flustered.

He strolled inside without her offering.

"Come on in," she said with an eye roll.

"You look red," he said, and removed his sunglasses. "You know, it's actually not good to take showers too hot. Cold showers are actually best."

She blushed an even deeper red. *If he only knew how much I could use a cold shower right now.* "Thanks for the tip," she said.

"So," he said, and sprawled on her couch. "What are you up to on your day off? Any hard and fast plans?"

She could have sworn he gave her a wink, but she wasn't absolutely certain. *Was he teasing? Was that supposed to be a double entendre?* She couldn't ever find her footing with him.

"Not really," she said, and sat on the chair opposite him. His eyes roved to her cleavage, and she pulled the robe tighter together.

"You know," he said, as he looked around, "I've never really looked around your place much. I'm usually in and out, you know."

Oh, God, I wish.

"It's cute," he said, and nodded his head. "It's you. I like these old buildings. All the wooden trim, the coffered ceilings." He got up and explored her picture frames. "This you?" he asked, and held up her senior group cheerleading photo.

"Yeah," she said, suddenly feeling like the awkward teen she'd been in that photo.

"Hot," he said. "I never hooked up with a cheerleader. Believe it or not, I wasn't such a ladies' man in high school. You still have the uniform?"

She turned scarlet. "Probably. Somewhere," she said.

"Huh." He continued to poke through her bookshelves. "Toni Morrison, J.D. Salinger, Sylvia Plath… Stephen King? That's an odd choice," he said.

"Don't knock it," she said, defensive of her books. "Regardless of genre, he's an amazing writer."

"I'm not knocking it," Connor said. "In fact, that would be my choice given your otherwise snobbish shelves."

"Snobbish? I don't go into your place and —"

"Calm down, pussycat, I'm just playing with you," he said. "But if you're trying to distract me from criticizing your books with a peepshow, you need to show just a little more skin." He nodded toward her thighs, and when she looked down, she saw that the robe had risen to almost entirely expose her lower half.

Hurriedly, Sam pulled the material together. "Is there something I can help you with? Besides random entertainment on your running break?"

He made his way back to her couch and sprawled out, feet kicked up on the coffee table. "Tell me what you think about the upcoming schedule," he said. "Any concerns? Requests? Specific restaurants or bars you want to go to? I can always ask James to move around the logistics. Hell, you might as well make the most of the gig."

She looked at him oddly. *Did he really run all the way over here to ask her if she had any changes to the schedule? And speaking of running, he'd have to* have *run a half marathon by now to get to her place!* "Hold on," she said. "Where exactly did you run from?"

He looked at his fitness watch and raised his brows. "What's it to you? I'm just trying to be nice, make sure you're happy with the schedule."

"Right, sorry," she said. "I'm fine with it, really. No complaints."

"And what about my father?" he asked. "I don't foresee any massive family gatherings coming up, but if you're uncomfortable around him —"

"I can handle him," she assured him.

"Handle him," he repeated.

"Yes."

"Hey, do you have any water? Diet soda?"

She groaned, but got up and headed for the kitchen. "LaCroix okay?" she called to him. "It's that or tap."

"God, you women and your overpriced French water crap. Yeah, that's fine. Do you have the blackberry cucumber flavor?"

She rolled her eyes and pulled one out of the box. "Yeah, women are the target demographic of LaCroix alright. And yes, I have it."

"Great. With a wedge of lime? In a glass?"

She brought them both a glass of the fizzy water, and held her hand over her chest to keep her cleavage discreet while she sat down. "I hope I'm getting a bonus for adding 'waitress' to my job description."

"Oh, I'm sorry!" Connor said, and sat erect. "How much do you think —"

"I'm kidding," she said with a laugh. "Calm down. Not everything has to do with money. But, you know, just for future reference, that's not how a polite guest acts."

"I didn't know I was a guest," he said as he took a long swallow from the glass.

"What else would I call you?" she asked.

He shrugged. "I don't know. A friend, I guess. That's how I talk to Chase and Jay and everyone when I'm at their places. Actually, with them, I know where everything is so I just take it."

"Oh," she said, and looked at her lap. *His friend?* She didn't know if that was better or worse than his employee.

"You know," he said, taking another sip. "The marketing behind this company really is genius. It's incredible they got so many people to slap down big bucks for what's basically carbonated water…"

She tuned out his words and just watched his body. Sam loved the way his incredibly long eyelashes contrasted with the rest of his body—everything else was so masculine, and yet there was that tiny touch of softness.

His jawline was incredible, looked like it was carved out of granite. With the shirt still sticking to him, she could recall exactly what his torso looked like naked, every swell and etching. *Big as a horse, the girl had said. Was it true?* She looked to his crotch and tried to visualize what was underneath. *What would be the harm in…*

"Sam?" he asked, and tore her out of her fantasy.

"Yeah, what? Sorry," she said. "I'm, uh, distracted today."

"I can see that," he said, knowingly. "But I'll let it slide this time. I can't expect you to always be on your A game. Especially when, you know, you're practically falling out of a robe."

She looked down again and saw her breasts were dangerously close to making a debut. "Shit," she said, and grabbed at the material.

"It's okay, I'm enjoying the show," he said with a smile. "But I should probably be going. I have a long run back."

As she stood up to walk him to the door, she realized he'd made her so sweaty that a droplet inched its way from her center down her inner thigh. When he turned to say goodbye to her at the door, it took all her willpower not to jump him.

"See you tomorrow," he said, and took off.

A sadness washed over her as she watched him leave. But at the same time, she couldn't wait to get back to herself.

She didn't even make it to her bedroom. Instead she sat on the couch, still warm from his presence, and finished herself off. The loudness of her cries surprised even herself, the wetness spreading across the leather.

As she reclined back on the cushions, she huffed. She'd hoped getting herself off would ease her horniness. But it just made her want him even more.

14

CONNOR

Be there in ten. His phone lit up with Sam's text, and he shifted uncomfortably in the seat.

"So, where's the wife-to-be?" one of the investors asked him pointedly, yet with a smile. Connor gave the older man with perfectly slicked-back hair his best charming grin.

"Almost here," he said. "She helped her mother with something this morning."

After all these years, he could still impress himself with how easily lies rolled off his lips. Especially when inside he was screaming at Sam. *Doesn't she know how many people would kill to be in the owner's box at a Redskins game?*

Why are you in an Uber? he texted her as he took a glass of ale from the waitress assigned just to them.

Car wouldn't start, don't know what's wrong with it, she replied.

He rolled his eyes. Connor had wondered if it would be okay if she drove herself. *What would be the harm? It's not like the investors would see that they arrived separately—and so what if they did? They weren't married yet.*

"I think it's sweet," the latest wife of one of the investors said. "You know, that you two aren't living together until after the wedding."

"I think it's stupid," her husband said. He was a man in his fifties, but Connor had to admit that he did a great job keeping fit. Marathons and cross-state cycling events gave him at least the suggestion that he deserved his wife, who was younger than his children.

"Hi." He didn't even have time to turn around before he felt Sam's hand on his arm. "My apologies. I was—"

"I told them you were helping your mother," he said, and pulled her close.

"Oh! Thank you, babe," she said. The waitress was already at her side, a sweating pint on her tray.

"Connor, I have to meet this pretty little thing." The oldest investor in the box ambled toward them, his hunched back somehow more grotesque given the twenty-two-year-old that was squeezed beside him.

He smiled. "Sam, this is Mr. Edmondson, one of the company's most revered supporters."

"He means holder of the company's deepest pockets," the old man said. He grinned lustfully at Sam. His eyes lingered at the tiny sliver of skin that was displayed between the tight designer jeans and Redskins jersey knotted above her navel. "You're lovelier than Connor—

and his father—mentioned," he said. His girlfriend squinted at Sam as she gauged the competition.

Sam smiled graciously and didn't flinch when he pulled her in for a cheek kiss instead of simply shaking her hand. "This how they make 'em these days, Connor?" he asked, though his gaze was directed at Sam's chest in the shiny tight jersey.

"It seems you already know that," Connor said as he deflected the attention back to Edmondson's girlfriend.

The old man looked up quizzically, glanced to the tight little blonde at his side and laughed. A full set of brand new, porcelain dental implants shone in the sun. "Right you are," he said.

Connor pulled Sam against him as he herded her around the box. As they made rounds, his hand slipped naturally to her tiny little waist, and his fingers brushed against the skin of her midriff. He was grateful for the excuse to wear jeans. They did a better job hiding his erection than suit trousers.

"Oh, honey, I hope you don't have babies too quickly," one of the wives said. She was one of the few well matched in age and pedigree to her husband. "Look at that figure. I used to have one like that. Remember, honey?" Her husband grunted, but stole what he must have thought were covert looks at Sam.

And she wowed them all. It wasn't just the feel of her body against him, or how the swell of her hips were the perfect perch for his hand. It was all of her. It also didn't help that she no longer stiffened up or paused like she used to during his play at advances. She rolled with it easily.

As the afternoon and game wore on, conversations about future investments at the company gave way to a more casual atmosphere. "Is there anything here that doesn't look like it was prepared by Gordon Ramsey?" she whispered to him after she'd turned down the last tiny gourmet appetizer.

"I think you need a Hoffmann's dog," he told her.

"What's that?"

"A hot dog with three additional types of pig on it. Bacon, sausage, and pulled pork."

She looked at him curiously. "I'd try that."

"Seriously? I can have the waitstaff—"

"No, after the game, can we go get one from out there?" she asked, and gestured to the exit.

"You mean where the commoners gather?" he teased her. "Let's go now, it'll just take a minute." He took her hand and looked around. "Would anyone else like a Hoffmann's dog?" he asked. The waitress immediately looked frazzled, and he held up his hand to her. "It's alright, we'd like to go."

All of the investors signed up for one, while the wives and girlfriends wrinkled their noses in a show of disgust. All except the solid older woman who no longer gave a damn what anyone thought of her. "Let them binge eat in secret after this," she whispered to Sam with a knowing smile.

As he led her out of the crisp, air conditioned suite, they took a shortcut through the stands. Suddenly, Sam pulled at his hand. When he turned around, she pointed to the field. They were hundreds of feet tall on the Jumbotron as the old-fashioned kiss cam graphics danced around them. Fans around them started to demand and chant that they kiss.

He leaned into her without even considering that she wouldn't oblige. When their lips met, the crowd thundered around them. One step behind and above him, she was at his height. He snaked his hands around her back and squeezed her ass, which he'd fantasized about mercilessly since that night at the underground fight. She filled his hands perfectly, and her eyes popped open in surprise.

"That should give the investors a show," he told her with a wink.

"This smells amazing," she said as they carried the signature dogs back to the owner's box. They'd stopped and picked up the red velvet chicken 'n' waffles for a touch of sweetness en route. "It almost makes up for my having to wear arguably the most racist shirt imaginable."

"Don't say that in the suite," he teased her. "You're making nice with some very rich people with some very strong opinions on why 'redskins' is still a perfectly acceptable slur."

The investors descended on the stadium food with gusto. The waitstaff scurried to refill pints while the wives and girlfriends picked gingerly at the food.

"You two look good together," the older wife told both of them. "We saw you on the big screen."

He watched Sam blush and put his hand on her leg. "I've been told I make some pretty solid decisions," he told the woman.

"Yes, well, my husband is quite taken," she said. "It's refreshing to see some youth and vigor revitalize the company. I imagine that will be reflected in a gesture of his soon."

Sam smiled at him as the woman moved on to compliment one of the young girls on her dress that looked painfully tight. Although it was just the two of them for a moment, he didn't move his hand from her thigh. She didn't seem to mind. He could feel the heat of her body, even through the denim, and wondered what she would do if he started to inch his hand up higher. Nothing? Uncross her legs? Give him permission with her eyes?

"Connor," one of the investors said. It snapped him instantly out of his daydream. "What do you think of their first-down running average? Obviously it's improved since the 2015 season, but I think…"

He squeezed Sam's leg, got up and moved to the investor to talk ball. But he felt her eyes follow him.

When the game was over and all the hugs and kisses were exchanged around the suite, Connor left last. He held the door open for Sam and indulged in a show of her hips swinging in those tight jeans. The ball cap that topped her ponytail and flawless old-school Adidas in custom burgundy and gold stripes were an impressive touch by James.

"Can I give you a ride home?" he asked.

She turned and looked up from her phone. "I was just ordering an Uber —"

He shook his head. "Don't worry about that, it'll take forever with the crowd. And premium parking is right here, so we can be out and I can have you home a lot faster than any Uber."

She bit her lip and looked at her phone again. "Well, if it's not too much trouble…"

"Not at all, come on," he said.

The attendant rushed to open their doors, and Connor got a kick out of watching what must have been a twenty-year-old kid ogle Sam as she slid into the car. "I didn't know you high rollers even had your own parking garage," she said. "And air conditioned, too."

"Only the best for people who spend thousands of dollars every year to sit in their tower above the field and barely watch the game," he said with a laugh.

"Not a huge fan, then?" she asked.

He shrugged. "It's alright. These things are just work for me, so it's not like I can enjoy them even if I really wanted to."

"Work, huh?" she asked with a smile.

He grinned at her and started toward the exit. "Yes, work. But who says you can't have some fun while you're at it?"

She lowered her cap as he paused at the gate to open the convertible top.

"Do you want to see my place?" he shouted to her over the wind. "We'll be driving near it."

"Sure!" she said.

He exited off I-395 and made his way to Lowell Street. Connor slowed in the familiar neighborhood. The last thing he needed was another complaint to the homeowner's association about how he "didn't drive like his kids lived here." One of the neighbors, a crotchety older woman who constantly tended her roses, gave the requisite wave.

"Is this your neighborhood?" Sam asked, almost in a whisper.

"This is it," he said. "And there's my place," he said as he pointed to the historic home which he'd had dramatically updated with touches of modern and mid-century modern flair.

"Are you serious?" she asked, wide-eyed.

"What, you don't like it?" he asked.

"It's just not what I expected," she said as she craned her head to watch it while they passed.

"What did you expect? Pink plastic flamingoes in the yard?"

"I don't know. More of a bachelor pad, I guess. A loft in the city."

"I'm full of surprises," he promised her.

15

SAM

"Well, this is a change," Connor said as he escorted her through the United States Botanic Garden. The setting sun was a swirl of pastel colors visible through the bubbled glass entry. "You're taking me out as arm candy for once."

"Oh shush," she said, but had to admit he was right. Her agency's annual summer celebration wasn't anything she'd looked forward to. However, when she'd realized Connor would be happy to use the opportunity for publicity, she started to look forward to it.

"What kind of look are you going for?" James had asked her via email. It was the first time she'd had any kind of say in her ensemble.

"Sleek, chic, but natural," she'd told him.

And he'd nailed it. She was draped in a knee-length yellow linen dress with artfully embroidered eyelets. It toed the line between sensual and feminine.

Sam took one of the walking appetizers and encouraged Connor to do the same. "What do you think?" she asked him. He finished the smoked salmon and violet tea delicacy in one bite.

"Delicious," he admitted.

She smiled. "That was my doing."

He raised a brow at her. "I'm impressed. Let's see what else you can do."

Sam made her rounds and got a little thrill every time she introduced him as her fiancé. For awhile, she'd resisted bringing the charade into her own life, but it was futile. There was no way she could keep up with the lies and stories. It was simply easier to let the worlds collide. Otherwise, she was sure she'd mess up, given how often Connor pulled her away for luncheons. Plus, when she'd found out Jenny couldn't make it, the situation became the perfect opportunity to show off.

Besides, what would happen if his family or business partners dug into her background and found out nobody in her life knew she was "engaged?"

"Sam, dear, your fiancé is a dream," Mrs. Whiteworth told her. "Though the name is familiar —"

"Everyone says that," he said quickly. "My family hosts a lot of events, but primarily business and personal affairs. I'm sure my mother's used your services before."

"That must be it," Mrs. Whiteworth said as she finished her glass of Prosecco.

Sam burned a bright red, touched his hand and scanned the crowd for an exit. "There are some clients I'd like to say hello to," she said to Connor. "Do you mind?" she asked Mrs. Whiteworth, who waved her away.

"I see you haven't built a foolproof backstory at work on how we got together," Connor said with a smile. "Is that frowned upon? Swooping in on heartbroken clients and snatching them up for yourself?"

"I don't recall anything about it in my contract," she said as her heart started to slow down.

"Hey, where are you actually taking me?" he asked as they left the crowd behind.

"I don't know."

The gardens seemed different at night, as the evening event lights worked their magic. The last time she'd been here, it was to survey the grounds and help plan this "little gathering" as her boss called it.

They moved from the lawn terrace and rose garden past the butterfly garden and toward the amphitheater. "I don't think I've been here since I was a kid," he said.

The two of them circled the empty amphitheater, drawn toward a hothouse. "Your mom used to bring you here?" she asked.

He laughed. "My mom? No. It was a school field trip. I don't recall my parents taking me anywhere that didn't serve them in some regard."

Connor tried the door of the greenhouse and looked at her with wide eyes when it opened.

"Should we?" she asked, and looked around.

"I think it's a sign."

Dim lights automatically flickered on when they entered, but they were so slight it was like being draped in moonlight. She could swear she could almost hear the plants sigh in their sleep. *Do plants dream? And if they do, what are we to them?*

She watched Connor explore the little nursery. He looked somehow both drastically out of place and just right in the tailored navy blue suit amidst all the greenery. "I used to come here quite often," she said. Sam wandered down the narrow aisle opposite of him. He looked up and caught her gaze over the sprawling leaves and beautiful blossoms.

"I can see that," he said.

"How so?"

"I don't know. It suits you. Being with all the flowers."

She blushed, grateful for the barely-there light. Here, in the greenhouse, it was like they'd built their own little world. Almost all of the sounds outside, including the chatter of the party, were silenced. Faintly, she could hear the jazz quartet as they played on.

Suddenly, she was very aware of her heartbeat. "They say plants and flowers respond to the sounds of music," she said.

"Who are they?"

"Who knows? Plant experts," she said with a laugh.

They each came to the end of their rows and faced one another. There was no longer a stretch of green to be used as a buffer. "I wish I'd come here more often," Connor said. "It's peaceful."

"It's an escape," she said.

"Yeah. I could have used that. I could use that," he said quietly.

"How come?" Her heart hammered into her ribs harder.

"Tough childhood," he said with a smile. "Though I'm sure you could have guessed that."

She looked at her feet. Her toes peeked out from the strappy golden Brian Atwood heeled sandals. "Your father?" she asked.

"Both of them. All of them. My mother isn't just depressed for the hell of it. She's an alcoholic—which, I'm guessing, is partially why my brother is, too. It started slowly, you know? I don't... I don't remember her drinking when I was very young. Or maybe I just didn't realize. Maybe she was better at hiding it."

Sam mulled it over. "I don't recall either of my parents ever drinking in front of me," she said. "Oh, once! There was this big party at my house. I was in junior high, and it was their twentieth wedding anniversary. My mom was tipsy on champagne, my dad on beer, and one of his friends pushed him into the pool." She laughed at the memory. "Somebody caught the perfect moment in a photo. The smile on his face was huge, even as he was inches from the water."

Connor smiled at her and moved closer. "I don't have any memories like that," he said. "I'm envious. My father—well, you know. The rageaholic, powerholic asshole. He was pissed as hell when I decided to enlist."

"I'm surprised he didn't stop you," she said. They walked side by side, slowly, around the greenhouse.

"He couldn't. I didn't tell him until after I'd signed up."

Her mouth fell open. "You didn't! I can't even imagine his reaction."

"I was scared shitless driving to the recruitment office. And driving back to my parents' house. I didn't know which was going to be worse."

"What did he say?" she asked. They came to a little bench, likely used solely for employees to rest. It was barebones and simple, with cascading green all around. He gestured for her to sit.

"My mother started bawling right away. My father, he didn't believe me at first. Said I was just trying to get to him. I mean, he was right," he said. "But he couldn't fathom that I'd gone all the way."

She shook her head in awe. "So, why the Navy? Why the SEALs?"

"I wish I had a more impressive or honorable answer for you," he said. "But honestly? It was the first office to call me back. And I knew a friend's older brother who was in the Navy, so that helped."

"Is that what you told the recruitment officer?" she asked with a smile.

"Hell no! I don't remember what bullshit excuse I came up with on the fly. Probably something about being a good swimmer."

"And is that true? That you're a good swimmer?"

"I am now," he said with a wink. "But I think in some regards the whole thing backfired. Don't get me wrong, I'm glad I served. And I'm thankful I was a SEAL. But it didn't take my father long to turn everything around and use my service as a platform to boast to his friends, colleagues and investors."

"That's terrible," she said.

"Honestly, I'm not even sure the extent of it. All I know is I left for basic, went all the way to SEAL training, made it through my first deployment—and when I got back, he'd gone full stars and stripes patriotic on me. Shit, you should have seen that first homecoming."

"What happened?"

"I didn't know what to expect. I'd been away from them for quite some time by then. I was a bit surprised he even allowed me back into the house, honestly. But when I walked in the door? It was like the flag had vomited all over the property and the place was stuffed with his friends. To this day, I don't think I can eat another blueberry and strawberry whipped pie."

She couldn't help but let out a little laugh.

"What's so funny?" he asked.

"Nothing, sorry," she said. "Your dad's a piece of work, but you have to give him credit for taking advantage of absolutely any situation."

He laughed with her. "He worked it, alright. You know Trezor quadrupled the number of political clients because of my father using me as an example?"

She eyed him closely in the soft light. "Do you feel a lot of pressure? Because of that?"

He looked surprised. "I suppose so. I never really thought about it."

"I dated someone, very briefly, who was an up-and-coming politician. I mean, very low ranks. Very young, of course, for a politician, but I think he had promise. But already he knew the importance of security."

"Are you talking about Alex?" Connor asked.

"How—how do you know about him?" she asked. "How do you know his name?"

He smirked. "You think I didn't do my homework? Although I have to admit, I was surprised to see someone without a background in modeling pop up in your dating history."

"You dug into my background?"

"Don't flatter yourself," he said, but knocked his leg against hers to let her know he was teasing. "James did. There were quite a few who were strangers to the catwalk! But, admittedly, a very generous sprinkling of models, too."

She blushed. "I doubt you're one to talk."

"I'm not denying that. Let's see, there was Samuel the medical resident, Alejandro the entrepreneur who made it on the *Forbes* list. Brett, Hunter, Colin, Andre, Jalen and Sourav were models. Then there was—"

"Okay, okay! I get it," she said with a laugh. "I get around."

"Yeah, you do!"

She flushed a darker shade and looked down. *If he only knew,* she thought to herself. *What would he think? What would he say if he knew with all those guys, I hadn't done a single thing with any of them? Would he be disappointed?*

Or would that turn him on?

CONNOR

Connor sat on the family plane and waited for Sam. He had to give her credit for her response for his last-minute invitation to Monaco. She rolled with the punches a lot easier now. Sure, she may have secretly flipped out, but her reply was fast, smooth and professional.

What do I need to bring? she'd asked.

He peered out of the Cessna 680 and caught sight of her being escorted by James. She ran surprisingly well in heels while James carried her leather duffel bag and white roller bag. Sam wore white linen pants and a matching breezy shirt with heavy, colorful beading at the neckline and oversized sunglasses.

She no longer looked like a hot girl he'd hired to play a certain part. Sam looked wholly natural.

"Hey," she said when she entered, just slightly flustered. "I made it!" She smiled warmly at him and pushed her sunglasses up and back to act as a headband.

He appreciated that, her smile. Although he'd do the same if their roles were reversed, he realized. She didn't have to, since there was nobody around who mattered. James tucked away her luggage and gave him a nod before he departed. The hired attendant briskly brought out a mimosa for her.

"So, why the sudden getaway?" she asked as she sat next to him and clinked glasses.

"Why not?" he asked. In reality, he figured he might as well make the most of the family plane before his rights to it were pulled. He still planned to leave the company. Connor just couldn't deal with being made the model figurehead in lieu of an actual, relevant leader.

But why bypass the perks while they were still within reach?

As the plane took off, she gazed out the window at Reagan's signature flight strip below. He felt the slightest pull at his chest. She looked like a kid in awe during her first flight. There was an innocence to her beauty he rarely noticed. Or maybe she'd just never let her guard down before. "You act like you've never been on a plane before," he teased.

She blushed and looked away. "I didn't realize private planes use major airports," she said, and sipped her morning cocktail.

"Sometimes," he said. "I prefer the services at major airports over the smaller ones. Even though, as you saw, even with the private parking facilities it can still be a bit of a pain to get here."

"It was fine," she said with a shy smile. "I've never been to Monaco. What's it like?"

"It's paradise," he said simply. The sun was fully visible, and with its rise it felt like they floated through the incredible violet sky.

Remember the contract, he told himself repeatedly as he watched her finish the drink as she took in the morning. *You promised yourself you wouldn't make a move. Why spoil a good thing?*

"You should get some sleep if you can," he said. "As soon as we land, we'll stop by the hotel to freshen up, then it's off to a night out."

"How long's the flight?" she asked.

"About nine hours. You're welcome to go stretch out in the back if you'd like."

She glanced toward the back of the plane, where the otherwise twelve-seater had been converted into six seats to make room for two sprawling beds covered with fluffy white down comforters. "You think of everything," she said softly.

"I can't take credit for this," he said. "This was all my father. Only the best," he said. Even he heard the twinge of hate.

"Are you going to sleep?" she asked.

"Maybe later."

After an hour, she got up and spread out on her side on top of the comforter. The attendant offered a silk eye mask, but she declined. Connor took another cocktail—

this one a scotch since it was past noon in Monaco, after all—and tried to bury himself in the news. It didn't work.

Eventually he went to the other bed himself. "Mask, sir?" the attendant asked.

"No, thank you," he said. "Do you mind some privacy?"

Without a word, she went to the front of the plane, pulled shut the privacy curtain, and it suddenly felt like just the two of them.

Connor half-shuttered the windows to allow in just a wisp of light. In the soft glow, he lay down and stared at the roof. His father had asked to have "galaxies overhead" and that's exactly what the creative team had done. Just a few feet above them, it was a virtual show.

Sam moaned lightly in her sleep, and he looked to her. God, she was beautiful, even as she slept. Her face was relaxed, lost in a dream. She was the kind of vulnerable you only saw in adults when they were asleep, and it made him feel protective of her. How could it be that he didn't even know her just a few weeks ago? And now here they were.

He felt drowsiness as it washed over him and fell asleep facing her.

Connor awoke with a dry mouth as the pilot announced their landing. He moved quickly to her bed and shook her lightly. "Wake up," he whispered. "You should see the landing."

Her eyes snapped open, those gorgeous green eyes alert and excited. "We're already here?" she asked, and he nodded.

"Oh my God," she whispered as the plane descended into Monte Carlo. "I get it now."

"Get what?" he asked.

She looked at him with big eyes. "Why the Monte Carlo in Vegas was designed like it is. It looks like it would fit in here perfectly. All white and regal."

He laughed. "I guess I can see that. I've never stayed at that Monte Carlo. I'm usually a Bellagio or Caesar's kind of guy."

"I've never *stayed* there," she said. "But I won twenty dollars with just a quarter in a slot machine there once." Her eyes were glued to the white sandy beaches and turquoise waters as they neared the little airport. "What do they speak here? French?"

"*Oui, tu as raison,*" he said. His French was rusty, and he'd always struggled to place his Rs in the back of his throat. Still, he'd persisted. It was good for business—and great for turning on women.

"*Remercier Dieu pendant quatre ans de français,*" she replied.

He looked at her, impressed. There were so many things he didn't know.

"Four years in college," she said with a grin.

He'd instantly hardened when she'd turned, so naturally, and that native-sounding French poured out of her mouth. *Don't let this get to you,* he reminded himself. Her excitement, how the language sounded on her tongue, the romance of being in Monte Carlo—it would be easy to get swept up in it. *Remember that we're going back. And the money that's between us. It's a business arrangement. That's all.*

"Thank you," he told the attendant and pilot as they departed, palming both of them a generous tip.

"Just renewed your passport?" the customs attendant asked Sam.

"Oh, yeah," she said.

"Nice picture," the small man said. *"Belle femme,"* he told Connor.

Parked with the engine running just past the small booth was the cherry red Alfa Romeo Spider 1600 he'd rented.

"Oh wow," she said as she traced her hand over the convertible. "A 1966?" she asked.

"Alright, what don't you know?" he teased her, and nodded for the hired attendant to take their larger bags ahead to the house.

"Who doesn't know that?" she asked. "Besides the fact that the Duetto is what Dustin Hoffmann drove in *The Graduate.*"

"Ah, Mrs. Robinson," he said. "One of my first crushes."

She looked at him with a raised brow.

"My father loved that movie," he said. "Big surprise. You want to drive?" he asked, and surprised even himself.

Her eyes got big. "No!" she said. "I… I don't like driving abroad. It makes me too nervous."

"Suit yourself," he said. The sun still lit up the sky, barely.

"Where are we staying?" she asked as she tied a silk scarf kept in her purse around her hair. She looked like a young Anne Bancroft, he realized. Save for those eyes that pulled everyone close.

"*Hôtel Hermitage Monte-Carlo*," he told her. He was slightly ashamed by how poor his accent was compared to hers. That was a first. It had been a long time since he'd felt bested by anyone.

"Never heard of it," she said. Sam's hand soared just beyond the door as she let the wind carry her. "Not that I expected to," she added.

"Well, it's no Monte Carlo in Las Vegas, but it should do," he told her. She slapped him lightly on the arm and laughed.

Sam took in the city with sheer wonder. He'd forgotten what that was like, to be so thrilled and awestruck at being somewhere new. To not feel like he had to act nonchalant and unimpressed with everything in life. Connor soaked it up happily and let himself experience the city through her eyes.

As they checked in, the man at the front desk eyed Sam without reservations. "Your, eh… sister?" he asked Connor. It seemed half in hope, and half in confusion that he'd booked a suite with two bedrooms.

"My fiancée," he said quickly.

"But, monsieur, you have the Exclusive Room," he said.

"Yes..."

"It has the, eh, two bedrooms? Are you expecting more guests?"

"No. We just like our space," he said. Sam had wandered away slightly and stared up at the soaring glass dome ceiling supported by elegant white columns which featured swirls and lattice-like details.

"Yes, I understand," the man said with a nod. "Pierre will escort you."

"Pierre," Connor whispered to Sam as they walked toward the private elevator. "Your boyfriend's here."

She rolled her eyes. "You caught me," she said.

"I can see you really do make full use of your French," he said.

As they crossed the foyer, a teenage boy on holiday with his parents meowed at Sam. She jumped and gave the kid a funny look. "What was that?" she asked Connor.

He laughed. "Meowing is the catcall in France. And, apparently, Monaco."

"Well, that's weird!" she said.

"Your suite," Pierre said, as he threw open the double doors in a grand gesture.

"Oh, my..." Sam's voice trailed off as she took in the incredible ocean views. "The beach is right there!" she said. Below them, the last of the setting sun was reflected in the waters.

"Would you like me to show you—" Pierre began, but Connor shook his head and handed him his tip.

"No need, I'm familiar with the suite," he said.

"It's incredible," Sam whispered to him. She stood at the glass that overlooked the beach, and he came up behind her.

"Go get ready for dinner," he said into her ear. "There are a few options beyond what James packed for you, waiting in your en suite."

"You're crazy," she said, but turned to him with eyes filled with wonder.

17

SAM

Sam had crashed right after dinner the night before, jet lagged and drained from the spikes in adrenaline. However, it ensured her clock got back on schedule and when she woke up in the morning, it was to a note from Connor which asked her to choose a bikini from the dresser for a day on the beach.

She couldn't help but try on every single one. From Minimale Animale sexy monokinis with mesh overlays to bright printed cutout bikinis from Agent Provocateur that made her feel like Sofia Vergara, she couldn't choose.

However, when she looked at herself in the mirror, shyness suddenly overtook her. She tried on a simple bikini, distracted by the fact that all of the bottoms James had chosen rode up her ass into makeshift G-strings. *Is this the look here?* she wondered.

"Connor! You out there?" she called.

"Yeah, you ready?"

"I don't know," she said. Sam walked out to the great room where sunlight streamed through the window. "I can't decide," she told him. "Which one do you think?" She held up the palm tree-covered mesh monokini and the option with bright pops of color and so many straps she couldn't remember how she got into it.

His eyes ate her up, and traveled from the span of her thighs up—slowly—to her throat. "Definitely the one you're wearing," he said lowly.

It made her blush, but she nodded and put the other two options away.

Even behind her Oliver Peoples glasses, she noticed the stares as they walked to the beach. "Isn't this a private beach?" she whispered to him as a middle-aged man's eyes nearly popped out.

"The hotel owns, it, yes," Connor replied. "But just because people have the money to stay here, it doesn't buy them any class."

She smiled and tucked a strand of hair behind her ear. Sam noticed how the blazing white bikini she'd chosen complemented Connor's trunks. The deep blue pattern was piped in white, and his vintage t-shirt was so tight in the arms and chest it threatened to burst.

"Wait a minute," Sam said. She slowed down and looked around the beach. "Are they... is she..."

"Who? What?" he asked, concerned.

Sam grabbed his forearm and pulled him close. "That woman over there is naked," she hissed.

"What? No, she's not," he said. He shaded his eyes with his hand and looked briefly. Connor turned back to her.

"Yes, she is!"

"She's *topless*," he conceded. "Not naked."

"That's what I mean!" Sam looked around and realized that most of them women wore nothing on top. Some were face down on their chaise lounge chairs or towels in the sand while they tanned their backs. But others didn't seem to give a damn and were proudly face up. A couple passed them and smiled in greeting. The girl's heavy breasts swung wildly.

"It's Monaco," he told her. "Most beaches here are topless. Hey, by the way, I got us a boat for tomorrow."

She smiled awkwardly at him and tried to regain her composure. Connor tipped one of the attendants as they reached a roped-off area of the beach. He spread out a massive towel for them and she began to rub sunscreen across her skin. "You mind doing my back?" she asked him as she handed the bottle over.

"That's an old line, if I ever heard one," he said, but Connor took the bottle.

She rolled her eyes behind her glasses. "It's hardly a line," she said. "That's exactly what I need, a sunburned back. Come on."

"Lie down," he commanded.

She moved onto her belly and rested her cheek on her hands. It felt strange, Connor's large hands on her shoulders. He massaged her shoulder blades, her "wings," as he called them, as slowly and seductively as possible.

Sam wanted to say something. She thought about breaking the tension by calling him out or making a joke, but couldn't seem to make herself speak. His hands on hers were like fireworks. She thought she might burst into flames if she spoke.

When his hands reached her waist, she could have sworn he squeezed gently. She felt his palms at the swell of her backside, his fingers at the hem of that tiny bikini bottom. Sam remembered just how slight that material was. She couldn't blame him if he stared at her ass, but was too embarrassed to turn around and look.

For a moment, she thought he would keep going. Just slide his hands underneath her, or into the crevice of her backside. But he stopped short. She was nearly breathless, and realized she'd hoped he'd go farther.

"Okay, now do me," he said. *Had she imagined the seduction? His voice sounded completely normal.*

She lifted herself onto all fours as he pulled the shirt over his head. Quickly, he rubbed the lotion across his chest and abs, legs, biceps and forearms. A tiny mewling came from somewhere nearby, and Sam looked around. She was shocked when she realized it was her, but Connor seemed too caught up in the task to notice. She'd never been more thankful for the sound of crashing waves, the only other sound that could mask what must have been sheer desire.

Connor flipped onto his stomach and handed her the bottle over his shoulder. She tried, awkwardly, to spread the white lotion across his shoulders and back, but he was just so broad.

"You're missing the other side," he told her gruffly. "You'll either have to switch sides when you're done or just get on. Don't worry, nobody's going to think you're assaulting me."

She blushed and weighed the options. It would be a look more awkward if she had to get up and do the other side when she was done. Sam straddled him, very aware of the seemingly sexual position. But nobody on the beach, either the other guests or the attendants, seemed to notice or care.

From this angle, his body was even more distracting. Her hands glanced across his muscled shoulders and lingered at his triceps which popped even when relaxed. She moved down and across his lats, feeling each swollen muscle at a time. "You could have been a massage therapist," he told her, his face buried in his arms.

Slowly, she worked down his back. The mound of his glutes was incredibly hard. She thought about what it would be like to be with him in *that* way. *I mean, a bunch of women already had, right? What did they know that she didn't?*

She thought of the girl at the party who'd congratulated her and compared him to a horse. All he'd have to do is turn over, and—

Sam realized she'd rubbed his upper butt for way too long. She wasn't sure how long exactly, but her imagination had whisked her away.

She got up abruptly, snapped the sunscreen shut and tossed it next to him. "I'm getting in the water," she mumbled quickly. He turned to look at her, and she thought she saw a glint in his eyes. Maybe? But no, it was the same Connor as always.

"If you're going out there, you may as well take your top off. You don't get those kinds of chances in the United States," he said. Then he smiled. "I can help you with the sunscreen in those hard to reach spots if you want."

She must have blushed all the way to her roots. "Are you crazy?" she asked. "And thanks, but no thanks on the offer."

"Okay, but look around," he said, and gestured toward the water. "You're going to stick out like a sore thumb."

She looked, and had to admit he was right. Not a single woman had her top on. *Haven't these women ever heard of monokinis or one-pieces?*

"Are you going?" he asked.

She shook her head and sat back down. "Never mind," she said. "It's not good to go out in the sun between ten and two anyway. That's when UV rays are the worst."

"You're making that up," he said with a laugh. Connor gestured for the attendant to bring them two drinks.

"I'm not!" she said. "Trust me, I once dated a dermatologist."

"Well, that's a sentence you don't hear every day," he said.

Sam dug a book out of her purse, turned onto her stomach and started to read.

"What are you reading?" he asked, almost instantly.

She sighed. "I'll let you know as soon as I figure it out."

He shrugged and went back to either texting or napping. It was incredible. He was surrounded by a ton of hot women literally wearing absolutely nothing but tiny bikini bottoms, and it was like he was completely oblivious.

Sam couldn't help but sneak looks at all the women as they passed. Of course she'd seen plenty of breasts in her life. The locker room, her girlfriends when they got ready together, but it was always very brief. Nobody just walked around and let it all hang out—literally—like that before.

Thank god for big sunglasses, because the people-watching here was incredible. All ages, all sizes, it didn't matter. She was particularly impressed by an older woman who must have been about sixty with the breasts of a teenager. "Hey," Sam whispered and nudged Connor. "Do you think those are real?"

"Huh? What?" he asked, and she realized he'd been asleep.

"Never mind," she said.

Another girl, who seemed quite young, wandered by and was painfully flat-chested. Sam felt sorry for her, but just for an instant. After all, it certainly didn't look like the girl lacked any self-confidence.

She sighed and looked down at her book. Her finger was still pressed into page three like a makeshift bookmark. *How long had they been out here?*

Sam pulled her phone out of her bag. She didn't have any data or service in Monaco, so it was really just a glorified clock. Nearly two o'clock. They'd been out here for hours. She'd been staring at strangers' tits for hours.

"Another drink, madam?" the attendant asked her. He was young, likely a teenager, with the most unbelievable bronzed skin.

"*Oui, merci,*" she said quietly. Connor breathed deeply next to her, but stirred at the brief conversation.

"Me, too," he said to her.

"Are you just waking up to eat and drink now?" she teased him.

"That's what a vacation's all about," he said. "By the way, you need to take some selfies or something and post them to whatever you do. Don't forget, we're still selling this. We'll call this the romantic vacation pre-wedding getaway project."

"Great," she said, but turned on her camera app. "Okay, act like you love me," she said and held the camera out to snap their photo.

She had to admit, he followed instructions well. They looked like any other happy couple. No filter needed.

"So, what was the book about?" he asked as the drinks arrived.

"Oh, um. Nothing you'd be interested in," she said.

18

SAM

When the sun started to set, they gathered up the towels and headed back to the hotel.

"I can't believe you didn't go in the water once," Connor told her.

She shrugged and tried to play it off. "Maybe tomorrow," she said.

"You hungry?" he asked.

"Starving. I thought for sure I could live off of mojitos, but apparently not. Twenty-one-year-old me is so disappointed in myself."

He laughed. "Well good, because dinner's in an hour. What are your thoughts on local oysters for a starter?"

Her stomach rumbled at the thought. Something about being in the sun all day had revved up her appetite. "Sounds great," she said.

They parted ways in the common area, and she sifted through the gowns and dresses that hung in her closet. She chose a floor-length, Grecian-style white gown with a slit nearly to her hip bone. It showcased her toned shoulders and the color she'd soaked up that afternoon.

In the shower, the six heads sprayed the last remnants of the beach from her. Sam watched white sand as it trickled down the drain. Just a few weeks ago, she never believed she'd be somewhere like this. *Thank god my job required me to get a passport to work there—just in case.* She'd been so nervous that Connor would realize she'd never been out of the country.

Sam swept her hair up in a loose chignon to show off the backless dress. Just a swipe of coral lipstick plus thick fake lashes, and the look was complete. There was no need for highlighter or bronzer. The beach had worked its magic.

She slipped into six-inch strappy metallic wedges and turned to check out every angle in the mirror. With the style of the dress, there was no way she could wear a bra or panties. However, nobody needed to know that to see how drop dead sexy she looked.

She smiled at herself in the mirror and walked into the common area. Connor was seated on the white leather sofa with a drink in hand. "Wow," he said. That was it. For once, she'd rendered him speechless.

Sam bit her lip. "I'm glad you like it. So… where are we going?"

"Here," he said. Connor stood up, pulled back the white curtain from their private balcony, and there was a candlelit table set with a lavish dinner.

"You had me get ready for this!" she said incredulously.

"I think it was well worth it," he said with a wink. He pulled out her rattan seat, and she felt his eyes on her chest as she sat.

As she sat across from him, nothing but candles and moonlight illuminated the balcony. The oysters were decadent, soaked in pink champagne, but something about the night quieted her appetite. Instead, they popped a bottle of champagne and clinked glasses. "I thought you were hungry," he said as he eyed her.

"I guess not as much as I thought," she said.

After they'd shared a bottle and picked at their food, Connor put his linen napkin aside. "Dessert?" he asked.

"What do you have in mind?" she asked coyly. He looked ravishing in a white suit with no tie and the top button of his pressed shirt undone.

"Come here," he said. "Let's enjoy it on the couch."

She settled across the cool leather and slid out of her shoes. The dress splayed out like a work of art. Sam *felt* like a goddess. As Connor returned from the kitchen with a silver platter of strawberries and freshly whipped cream, she hoped he thought so, too.

"They're local, from Strawberry Fields Farm," he said as he sat next to her.

"That name sounds made up," she said.

"If it were, I'd have come up with something more creative," he said. He picked up one of the largest berries and held it to her lips. Sam caught his eye and held it as she bit into the juiciness. It was at the peak of ripeness, and the sweetness ran down her chin.

Before she could react, Connor wiped the juice from her jaw and brought his hand to his mouth. He licked the juice from his thumb and put the tray aside.

She leaned into the kiss before she was even certain it was happening. His hand cupped her chin and controlled her. With her head lifted toward him, his lips were on hers and she could taste nothing but the sweet berry.

When his tongue slipped between her lips, she let out a moan. Her back was arched, her chest pressed up against him. Connor's hand found her thigh instantly. He explored the stretch of silky skin, and slowly moved higher. He dragged out every moment.

Sam slid his jacket off his shoulders hungrily while he grabbed her thigh and draped it across his lap. His hand traveled higher as he kneaded and squeezed every part of her leg.

When he reached her hip, she felt him search for her underwear and she laughed into his mouth. "Nothing there," she said.

He grinned and squeezed her ass as he pulled her on top of him. As she straddled him, she could feel his hardness between her legs. She was already wet, but couldn't help grinding against him. Even through his trousers, she got a hint of what that girl had meant by "built like a horse." But Sam was so turned on, it no longer intimidated her.

Connor's mouth moved from her lips to her jaw and traveled to her neck. The heavy jewels of the dress' neckline stopped him. With one hand—the other still firmly on her backside—he reached behind her and unhooked the neck of the dress. It fell quickly around her waist and exposed her breasts.

A part of her felt suddenly shy, but Connor held her at arm's length to admire her. "You're even more beautiful than I imagined," he said.

His hand snaked below the folds of the dress, which was now solely held against her body at the waist, and he bolstered her up above him so her nipples met his mouth. She felt his fingers digging into her cheeks, dangerously close to her opening as the warmth of his mouth consumed one nipple and the next.

Sam whimpered as she felt her nipples harden against his tongue. She wanted desperately to be lowered, to be able to rub herself against his hardness again, but he kept her firmly poised inches above his lap.

She squirmed, and his hands that clutched her bare ass shifted closer to her center. His fingers spread her apart. The ache of emptiness was unbearable. "Fuck, you're wet," he told her between sucks on her nipples.

"Stop teasing me," she said, frustrated.

"Is this what you want?" he asked as he lowered her back down. Instead of letting her go completely, he slid a finger inside her and pushed his thumb against her clit. She shuddered at the surprise of it—and the pleasure of having some part of him inside her.

Sam couldn't bring herself to reply, but moved against his hand eagerly. His movements were skilled, with practiced flicks against her G-spot and just enough pressure on her clit to get her halfway to orgasm. But no closer.

She kissed him deeply, eyes squeezed shut. All she wanted was to come.

"Slow down," he told her.

There was a part of her that thought maybe he'd just stop. Maybe it was all just a game, a power trip. She rode his hand harder, lifted her head and offered her breasts to his lips again. He spanked her once, hard. "I said slow down," he said.

The slap surprised her, but even as the sting faded and she felt her ass turning red, she also felt a new gush of wetness between her thighs.

Connor slipped his finger out of her and flipped her onto her back. The coolness of the couch was a shock to her skin. He knelt and spread her legs wide. "You didn't let me have any dessert," he told her. "That's not very nice."

She smiled and let her head fall back as he kissed his way up her thighs. When he reached her mound, he kissed his way across it and trailed his tongue against her skin. He came so close to tasting her, really tasting her, and yet pulled back.

Sam shook her head back and forth, ready to burst. "What do you want?" he asked her.

"Connor, please," she said and arched her back as far as she could.

"You're going to have to tell me," he said.

She worried her lip and he blew on her clit lightly. "I want you to eat me," she said.

His tongue ran across her clit, firm and slowly, before it dipped down into the deepest of her folds. She cried out and dug her fingers into his hair to hold him closer to her. As he worked his tongue faster, she couldn't stop calling out his name. When he slid a finger into her again, she reached for her breasts and pinched her nipples.

She didn't want to come, not like this. "I want to taste you," she said, breathless. He pulled his finger from her and left a flutter of kisses on her clit.

"What about the contract?" he asked, even as he unbuckled his trousers and she slipped completely out of the dress.

"Consider it on hold for the weekend," she said.

When he revealed himself to her, she knew instantly the girl hadn't been lying. She'd never really *seen* one before, not really, but he was huge. Still, that ache that throbbed deep inside of her didn't stop.

She reached for him, but he stopped her. "Like this," he said, and took the whipped cream from the abandoned tray of strawberries. Connor spread the cool sticky slickness across her breasts—and along his shaft. He straddled her chest and took her hands. "Press your tits together," he told her.

As soon as she did, he slid his cock between her breasts and the tip into her mouth. Sam licked and sucked at him like she was starved. The heat of his length between her breasts and the sweetness of the cream blended with his own taste was intoxicating.

He kept one hand loosely on her head and caressed her cheek while he watched her take him deeper and deeper into her mouth. He rose up, brushed her hands away from her breasts, leaned down and kissed her. He lapped up every last part of the cream, from her lips to her swollen nipples.

"Every part of you tastes so good," he said. She wanted to tell him the same, but her jaw ached and her lips were numb from sucking just the couple of inches he gave her.

Standing up, he scooped her up in his arms easily.

She laughed. "What are you doing?"

"I want to fuck you properly," he said and carried her into his bedroom.

19

CONNOR

The way she looked at him when he tossed her on the bed, was with a degree of lust he'd never seen before. Her green eyes pulled him in.

When he penetrated her, she was shockingly tight. He'd been with women before who were religious about their kegels. He'd even been with one girl who'd had her vagina "reconstructed" so that she was supposed to feel like a virgin again. But none of them came close to how tight, how wet, and how addictive Sam was.

"Are you okay?" he asked her. She'd bristled when he entered her, but still writhed against him. "Is it okay to keep going?"

"Yeah, yes," she breathed into his ear. "Please… I want you to fuck me."

He buried his face in her neck and breathed her in. Connor was used to the looks when women first saw him. He knew he was big—that must be all it was. He took his time and slid in and out of her slowly.

When he teased her, lingered with barely his tip inside her, she struggled and demanded that he go deep. Every time he slid against her G-spot, she scratched at his back and cried out his name.

She was so wet it was almost unbelievable. "Get on top," he told her. "I want to watch you."

On his back, he watched her straddle him. Her hair had come undone and hung in knotted waves over her breasts. He reached up, pushed the hair aside, and pulled her nipples. She looked down and grasped his cock to place him at her opening.

Connor moved his hands to her hips. He loved to control women from here, when they thought they had all the power. "Slowly," he told her. She'd let her weight fall onto him, but he held her up. He wanted to watch her take him in.

"Please," she whispered when he was halfway in. He pulled her down, hard, onto him, and she called out.

Her nails dug into his chest and he clutched her ass as she rode him. She was perfect. Her breasts bounced wildly. Every part of her skin felt like silk. Sam's wetness was so intense it dripped down between his own thighs.

Her eyes were closed and she ground hard against him. "Look at me," he told her. She opened her eyes and he could tell she was close.

Connor pushed himself up and wrapped her legs around his back. From here, he was in complete control—and her nipples were once again aligned with his face. They were perfect with light brown areolas and tight little nipples. He lifted and lowered her onto his cock while he covered her chest in marks he knew would darken to hickeys by the next day.

Her legs were locked around him, his lap soaked with her juices. "Connor," she gasped out. "I'm going to come…"

He could feel her orgasm start to wash over her as the heat of her insides throbbed. It was enough to push him over the edge and he came with her. When he exploded inside her, she screamed out louder.

It wasn't what he'd expected or what he'd planned, not that he'd planned any of it. But he'd never come inside anyone before. Hell, he'd never had unprotected sex with anyone but Sandra before. There was something special about Sam, though.

She shuddered against him as she rode out the last of her orgasm. He kissed her neck gently and made his way to her lips.

Connor leaned back and lightly trailed a hand across her clit, though he was still inside her. She shook and laughed.

"Too sensitive," he said.

"I, um. I've never done that," she said.

He held her hips and pushed into her once more, just to watch her shake as a small tremor of an aftershock rocked through her. "I wouldn't exactly call it a one-night stand," he said with a laugh.

"No, I mean… never mind," she said, and pushed off of him.

"The no protection thing?" he asked. "Sorry, me either. Not really. But I'm clean, I just got tested a month ago."

"It's not that," she said. Sam perched on the edge of the bed, grabbed a tissue from the nightstand, and wiped up their combined juices from between her thighs.

"Then what is it?" he asked. "I mean… you didn't like it?"

"No!" she said and looked at him, shocked. "It was amazing. Everything I'd imagined." She blushed at that, as if she thought it had really been a secret that she wanted him. "It's just… I've only been with one person before."

"Yeah, right," he said with a laugh.

"I'm serious!" she said. "Sexually, just one person. And… well, just one time."

"Wait a minute," he said. "What do you mean one time? And what about all those models —"

"They're just for fun," she admitted, her head hung low. "We flirt and sometimes we kiss. Not much. But that's about it."

"But you weren't a virgin, right? I mean, I wasn't —"

"No. Technically, no, I wasn't a virgin. But… shit, this is embarrassing," she said.

"Hey," he said as he wrapped an arm around her. He suddenly felt protective. "It's okay. You don't have to tell me anything."

"No," she said with a sigh. "I want to. So, when I was sixteen, I had sex with my high school boyfriend. Kind of. It was terrible. Almost traumatizing."

He looked at her, concerned. "Did he do something? Did he—"

"No! No, nothing like that. We were just, you know, kids and inexperienced and everything. It lasted maybe two minutes, max. I don't really remember much after he… well, you know, tore my hymen… just a lot of pain and then it was over."

"So, why did you … why was it only the one time? If he was your boyfriend?"

She looked at her lap, ashamed, and pulled the sheet around her chest in a makeshift toga. "We 'dated,' if you want to call it that, for about six weeks before that night. He was older, a quarterback on the varsity team. I was just a sophomore. He wasn't faking the relationship with me, not really. But…"

"But what?" he asked.

She looked at him, and he knew all her walls had fallen down. "He told *everybody*," she whispered. "Everybody. The next day at school, everyone knew."

He let out his breath. Connor had known guys like that in school. He hadn't been one of them, but more than once he'd laughed along as a buddy had shared his latest conquest. "I'm sorry, Sam," he said.

She shook her head and let out a small laugh. "It's not your fault."

"But that was a long time ago. Do you think that's why it was just that one time? Or…"

"I don't know," she said with a shrug. "I'm sure that certainly didn't help. But I also just never felt comfortable with anyone. You know? Don't worry, it's not like I was holding out for 'the one' or anything," she said with a smile.

He grinned and looked away. Connor had to admit, there was a part of him that had started to suspect that. The strange thing was, he liked it. It humbled and honored him. *What's the matter with me?*

"I, well, I wish I would have known," he said. "I would have, uh, been a little gentler. I suppose."

"I liked it," she said.

"Yeah, I could tell," he said, and nudged her with his elbow.

She giggled. "What can I say? That's what years of sexual suppression and build-up will do to you."

Connor lay back on the bed and pulled her down with him. She curled into his chest with an arm and leg spread over him. It felt natural, easy. He'd never been one for cuddling after sex, and usually merely tolerated it, if anything. But with Sam it wasn't just about the sex. That had been phenomenal, but there was something more between them.

"So," he mused. "Contract's suspended for the weekend, huh?"

"That was my executive decision," she declared.

He felt himself start to harden again. It was the press of her breasts against his chest, and the wet heat against his thigh. *What the hell? We've already fucked once, what could another time hurt?*

He ran over every possible justification as he leaned down and kissed her again. She responded instantly and ran her hand across his chest. Still, he was worried. There were feelings stirred up in him that went much deeper than lust. *You're going to screw everything up.*

But he couldn't stop himself. She'd reached down and had stroked him into full hardness. As Sam kissed his neck, down to his stomach and straddled his thigh as she took him into her mouth, he just couldn't stop it.

She felt amazing, every part of her. Sam gripped his base while she took him deeper into her mouth toward her throat. He gasped out. Already she was riding him at his leg, and her juices dripped down his thigh.

Connor opened his eyes and watched her. She worked him like a pro for this basically being her first time. Of course it couldn't be, not with her this comfortable about it. He couldn't help but be doubtful.

"You give head like a pro," he told her.

She smiled up at him and licked the length of his shaft.

"This your first time?" he asked her.

She nodded. "But I'm not going to lie," she said with a slight blush. "I've watched my fair share of porn."

So that was it. The idea of her watching porn while she got herself off made him even harder. He wanted to watch her, to see how she handled herself. "When was the last time?" he asked her.

She flicked her tongue across his tip. "Last time what?" she asked.

"The last time you got yourself off watching porn," he said as he raked her hair back and held it in a fist behind her head.

She turned red. "Um, well, you kind of interrupted me," she said.

"What do you mean?" His cock throbbed, begged for her mouth, but the curiosity was stronger.

"Remember the time you came to my house unannounced on your run?"

"You're kidding," he said as he sat up. "You were…"

"Yeah. Okay?" she asked, embarrassed.

"Don't be embarrassed, it's hot as hell," he said. "I just wish I would have known."

"Why?" she asked with a smile as she stroked him gently. "What would you have done?"

"Probably something like this," he said, and he grabbed her quickly to pull her up to him.

She squealed, but her sounds quickly turned to moans as he entered her again. Immediately, he was struck again by just how tight she was.

"I could fuck you all day," he told her as their rhythms synced up.

"I dare you," she said. She closed her eyes and tilted her head back. Her long hair brushed across his legs.

He'd never seen anything so beautiful in his life.

20

SAM

When she awoke, it took her a moment to realize where she was. Although the entire weekend was already a blur. Sam turned on her side and felt the white silk sheets against her naked body. Connor was nowhere to be seen.

She reached out and felt his spot, still warm and wrinkled. From the other room, she heard him say, "Right in here."

An older man in an intricate uniform pushed a trolley into their bedroom, and Sam scrambled to make sure the sheet covered her bare breasts.

Connor laughed. "Don't be so modest, they've seen it all."

She smiled awkwardly as the man ticked off the breakfast items, but she was so self-conscious she didn't hear anything. Connor thanked him and crawled back into bed with her. He wore nothing but a towel wrapped around his waist.

"I wasn't sure what you'd like," he said. He smiled at her almost shyly, like a teenager.

"I'm starving, it all smells good," she said. Sam cut into the eggs Benedict and watched the perfectly poached yolk spread across the plate.

Connor tore apart a plate of crepes full of local berries and fresh whipped cream. She blushed and took a long swallow of grapefruit juice when she remembered their last encounter with cream.

Sam set the plate aside and flopped onto her back. She was sore, incredibly so, between her legs and her chest ached from all the attention. "So," she said. "What's the agenda for today?"

"This," he said simply and pushed the entire trolley aside. "And maybe some of this," he said, as he slid his hand under the sheet and lifted it. "Jesus, what happened to you?"

She looked down and saw that her chest was absolutely covered in hickeys—and the occasional bite mark. "*You* happened," she said. "I'm certainly not going anywhere topless now!"

"Outside the bedroom, you mean," he smirked at her.

"Be serious," she said. "What do you have planned today?" She was dog-tired, but she wouldn't admit that to him.

"I am serious," he said. "What's wrong with spending the day in bed?"

"Nothing," she said as she chewed her lip. "But won't they... won't they talk?"

"Who?" he asked, confused.

"The staff and everybody."

"Oh, right. And what do you think they'll say? Get a room? I already did!"

"You're crazy," she said, and rolled her eyes.

"Not crazy, just still hungry," he said. Connor slipped down below the sheets and nuzzled his face between her legs. "You have anything for me?"

The next morning, she got up before him and tiptoed into the shower. Warm water was just what she needed to soothe her aching muscles, not to mention wash the sweat and their combined juices off her body. Sam glanced in the mirror and almost jumped.

She had the most insane sex hair she'd ever seen, and the makeup that lingered from that first night had created a sensual smudged look at her eyes. The hickeys were already faded somewhat, but anyone could look at her and tell what she'd been up to for the past thirty-six hours.

Damn. Had it really been that long? But she couldn't get enough of him. And clearly, the feeling was mutual.

Sam turned the water on nearly as hot as it would go and stepped into the steamy glass box. She lifted her face to the shower head and closed her eyes. *This is all a fairy tale. One that's coming to an end really soon,* she reminded herself.

Surely they weren't the first people to get caught up in the bubble of Monaco.

"Hey shower hog," Connor said to her as she emerged from the bathroom. One Turkish towel was wrapped around her head and a thick fluffy robe drowned her.

"I blame you," she said.

"Can you be ready in an hour?" he asked.

"Sure, what's up?"

"We're heading out on the water," he said. "I figured breakfast al fresco on the deck would be a nice change of pace."

"Don't tell me," she said as she towel-dried her hair. "You have a gilded white yacht with some pompous name like the White Swan docked just down the beach."

"It's not gilded, it's trimmed in mahogany," he said. "And I'd never name her the White Swan! How girly do you think I am?"

She was a bit taken aback. Honestly, she'd thought he'd rented a yacht at best. "So, uh, what's her name, then?" she asked.

"Sophia Lure-In," he said with a straight face.

"You've got to be joking," she said.

"L-U-R-E hyphen I-N. Get it?" he asked. "Plus, she's only the hottest woman I ever saw. Besides you, of course," he said with a wink.

"Yeah, I get it," she said with a laugh. "Just not what I expected."

"I need to shower," he said, and smacked her butt as he walked by. "The assault on your tits is looking better. Is it a topless kind of day?" he called as he turned on the shower.

She didn't reply, but that was a consideration as she considered which swimsuit to wear.

"This is amazing!" she said as they set sail on the gem-colored water. "I didn't know you could navigate a boat."

"It's really not that hard," he said. "The most challenging part is keeping in communication with the other seafarers. And, you know, avoiding the drunk boats."

She leaned against the rich mahogany wood and popped a frozen grape into her mouth. "I expected you to have a fleet of servants or something on board," she said. "With their little white gloves and everything."

"Is that what you think of me?" he asked. Connor looked at her with what she thought was a slightly pained expression. "I hire help when it's necessary. But really, I prefer not to be pampered and swaddled like a child when I can help it."

"Sorry," she said quietly.

All around them, a handful of yachts sailed by along with plenty of smaller boats. There was a generous sprinkling of jet skis, kayakers and stand up paddleboarders, too. "I'm going to try and get us away from the tourist area," he said, and navigated the yacht toward the open water. "Go on up, I'll meet you there in a minute."

Above deck, she stood at the helm of the ship and stretched her arms out. *Might as well get my* Titanic *moment in before he sees me,* she thought. Eyes closed, all she felt was the sun on her skin and the gentle mist of the warm water splashing up from below.

"Show me your tits!" a voice called from far away. Her eyes snapped open and she dropped her arms. About fifty feet away, a group of guys who appeared to be in their twenties with fishing gear were in a little boat and staring at her.

Sam didn't know what got into her, but she lifted up her fringed bikini top and smiled. They started to holler and cheer. She'd never felt freer.

"I see your modesty has gone overboard." She turned and saw Connor behind her. He grinned at her as she went to lower the bikini top. "No, no, please don't on my account." She cocked her head, then removed the top completely.

"Fucking score, man!" one of the guys yelled to Connor, but by now their boats had sailed far from one another. She glanced around, but couldn't see any other boats close enough to make out the people on board.

Connor approached her and she saw his erection through his trunks. He grabbed her waist and pulled her close. "You like putting on a show?" he asked.

"I don't—"

"Turn around," he said. She did as he instructed and felt his hands on her stomach. Both at the helm of the ship, he unbuttoned her cutoff shorts and slid them down her thighs. When they hit the floor, she stepped out. Sam could feel his hardness against her hip.

With one quick motion, he untied the bikini bottoms like a gift and tossed them aside. Connor wrapped one arm around her chest and began to fondle her breasts. His other hand wandered to what he thought would be the small landing strip she normally shaved into her mound. He felt nothing but skin.

"Naughty girl," he told her.

She smiled. "I thought you'd like the surprise. I did it this morning."

He tested her clit for a response and she gasped. Next, he worked through her folds to gauge her wetness. "You're fucking insatiable, aren't you?" he whispered into her ear. "Taste this," he said, and brought a finger to her lips. It was coated in her juices.

While she sucked on his finger, she felt him drop his trunks. Connor pressed on her back. She leaned forward and grasped the railing. He entered her quickly, his hands clutched to her hips and thumbs dug into the dimples of her back.

Sam watched the turquoise waters rage against the slick whiteness of the boat. Connor grabbed her hair, which whipped around her face, and knotted it in his fist. He forced her head slightly up, and she saw there was a smaller yacht approaching. "Connor—"

"Don't stop," he told her.

She kept an eye on the boat as it approached. When she caught sight of a couple, likely in their thirties, she thought she'd crumble. But instead it turned her on, and his cock that pounded into her felt even more incredible. The couple were in lounge chairs, but sat up. The woman, a slender redhead, poked at the man. He lowered his sunglasses to look at them.

"They're watching," she told Connor. Her heart hammered. If the boats got any closer, she was sure she'd make real eye contact with them.

"And what do you think of that?" he asked her. She felt his palm meet her ass and she yelped.

Sam smiled. "I like it," she said.

She couldn't be certain, because the boats had started to pass, but she thought she saw the woman reach for the man's crotch. One thing was certain—they'd definitely started to make out.

"Come in me," she said, loudly to be heard over the water.

As if he'd been waiting for permission, he let go inside her. His come slammed against her G-spot and brought her over the edge.

They fell into their own lounge chairs farther back on the deck. She no longer felt any sort of embarrassment with her naked body. In fact, she'd never felt more alive in her life.

"You're incredible," he told her.

She watched him as he slipped on sunglasses and nothing else, and gazed into the distance.

Maybe this isn't so crazy, she thought to herself. *Maybe we can really do this, for real. What was the big deal?*

She could handle his family, no problem. And Connor's occasional mood swings and arrogance. Underneath, he really was a softie.

They enjoyed each other's company, right? It wasn't just the sex. Sam began to feel a genuine pull of emotions as she pictured them together. It was dangerous, she knew, but only natural. And he had to feel the same way. Didn't he?

I mean, crazier things have happened, she thought to herself.

21

CONNOR

He didn't know where the time went. Their long weekend was already over, and yet that plane trip across the ocean seemed like ages ago.

Connor held Sam close as she slept, their bodies curved into each other. *Four days just isn't enough,* he thought to himself. She stirred and murmured in her sleep. He leaned down and smoothed her hair while he kissed her forehead.

The sex was amazing, there was no doubt about that. But he'd had fantastic sex before.

This was more. Deeper. There were little signals he shouldn't have ignored going into this, but he'd thought it was just infatuation.

Connor wasn't used to being wrong.

He carefully untangled himself from her warm body and slipped onto the balcony. Connor closed the French door behind him and slumped into the wrought iron chair with the plush down cushion.

He lit a cigarette, a rare occurrence and one of the few bad habits left from his high school days. As he inhaled deeply he watched the full moon as it lit up the evening waves—and the nude couple in the waters who thought nobody watched.

Someone's always watching, he thought to himself.

Connor leaned forward and looked at Sam, belly down on the bed with one thigh hiked up high. She was an absolute vision. And the strangest part was, he didn't think she faked it. She seemed to really like him, regardless of his fortune.

You need to break this off, he told himself. *First thing in the morning, a serious talk needs to happen. Fuck. If you were going to screw her at all, it should have just been the once.*

He knew that was just hopeful talk though. Once would never have been enough.

Connor turned his phone off of airplane mode for the first time on the trip and watched the emails, texts and Snapchats come through. A girl whose name he didn't even remember had sent him a selfie of herself topless. Her breasts were painfully swollen with silicone.

Another girl had sent him an email which he didn't even open. The subject line read, "I've been thinking about you..."

None of them did anything for him. He scrolled through a few more texts from women he'd taken out once or twice. Some of them he'd slept with, others had done a shit job of acting like they were more modest than that. All the photos were charged with sex, from the lingerie-clad selfies to the ones who pretended they didn't know their tits practically fell out of their dresses.

None of them were Sam.

He groaned and rested the cigarette in the ashtray. *I'm not ready to feel so deeply for someone,* he thought. Especially the girl he'd hired to be his fake fiancée. No matter how deep these feelings were, he needed to put an end to it. *It's for the best.*

And it started right now. He looked to Sam again, but couldn't be the guy who woke her up in the middle of the night while she was still naked to break it off. Connor had at least a little more compassion than that.

Instead, he opened up his favorite "dating" app and started swiping. It was a joke people even called it a dating app, but it had made his life a hell of a lot easier when the app was developed. For a little while, he'd toyed with making some of the girls he met up with think he was average in every regard. Average job, average income, average family and average cock.

But they always found out the truth. Only twice had he used a completely fake name so they couldn't look him up, and he'd felt so slimy he never did it again. Just one of those girls he'd slept with had ruined it for him. Hearing her shout, "Curtis!" over and over was a real buzzkill.

He'd discovered that while his money and background certainly sped up the process, it wasn't necessary to lead with. Connor was popular with women online and in real life. It was his looks, the way he'd learned to tell women what they wanted to hear, and of course what he packed in his jeans.

Still, the app was like a shortcut. He still loved the thrill of the hunt, and there was something about meeting a woman in a bar. The way they looked like prey, like little white rabbits that begged to be cornered.

However, in recent years, he'd noticed women had increasingly approached him. He appreciated it, sure, but it definitely dulled the excitement. Also increasingly, the women were older. Connor didn't mind cougars, in fact before Sam they'd been some of his best experiences —but it was also off-putting.

What are you going to do? Walk down to the hotel bar right now and pick someone up? He couldn't be that shitty.

Connor turned his back completely to Sam. He almost wanted her to wake up and catch him as he swiped right over and over. Then it would be easy. She'd be the one to break things off. He didn't even register any of the women's photos, let alone their bios. All he could think about was Sam.

How bad would it be to wake her up to fuck her just one last night? Too bad, he decided. That was almost his father's level of disgusting. Still, he knew she wouldn't mind. *What if she woke up already close to orgasm?* No, too creepy. He just couldn't do it.

He wanted her more than anything. No matter how many times they had sex, it just wasn't enough. More like a temporary satiation that they both knew wouldn't last. And still, in between those sessions, it was fun.

Relaxed. Comfortable even. *Is this what it's supposed to be like?*

Part of him also wondered how much of this she was faking, if any of it. After all, he'd propositioned her to be a contractor for him the day they met. And he'd been a raving lunatic that day over Sandra. *Maybe she's pretending with all of this. Maybe she's going to blackmail me!*

Connor looked at her again at that thought. *No. You're just being paranoid,* he told himself. Nobody was that good of an actor. In bed, she was wild, and he knew she wasn't just making up the whole story about him nearly being her first time. He'd never felt anyone that tight before. Not even when he'd been in high school himself.

Clearly, she was genuine. But if that was the case, what did she want with someone like him?

He forced himself to actually look at the photos at least before he swiped. Sure, some of them were cute. Some of them were hot. However, even without taking rampant photo manipulation out of the equation, they just didn't get him hard the way Sam did.

What are you up to tonight? One of the women had already messaged him. He realized it was just early evening back in DC.

Sitting on a balcony in Monaco with my fake fiancée naked in bed a few feet away. That certainly wouldn't go over well. *Shit, you can do this! What's your problem?*

Looking at your gorgeous pictures while I'm away on business, he replied after ten minutes.

He got a winky face in return. This one was already in the bag. She was young, curvy and blonde with a bachelor's degree in communications. She mentioned in her bio she was an administrative assistant at some tech company he'd never heard of. And obviously, she had no qualms about making the first move at what was an early Friday evening for her. Easy. *Damn, your friends are right,* he thought to himself.

"Come back to bed." Sam's voice shook him out of his inner struggle. He glanced behind him and she was propped up on the bed with the blanket draped across her legs.

He looked back to the app and saw the woman had started to type more. Connor clicked it off, set the phone on airplane mode, and went back inside.

"What were you doing?" she asked sleepily.

"Watching a couple of people fuck in the ocean," he said.

"Ew, were you smoking?" she asked and wrinkled her nose.

"When in Monaco," he said. Connor pulled off his shorts and got into bed with her.

"You didn't shut the doors," she said as he kissed her neck.

"So then you might not want to scream too loudly," he replied. *Hell, one more time couldn't be too terrible, right?* He reached up and turned the lamp on.

"What are you doing?" she asked. Sam squinted as her eyes adjusted.

"I just want to see you," he said. She smiled that sleepy smile at him.

Connor worked his way down her entire body. He memorized every freckle, every curve and every taste. He wanted to remember the exact saltiness of the inside of her elbows, and how the tiny birthmark at her ankle looked vaguely like a horseshoe.

"Am I getting the romantic treatment now?" she asked when he kissed his way back up and lingered at the widest part of her hip.

He didn't reply. Instead, he moved away and flipped onto his back. "Here," he said, and gestured to his lips. "Sit here."

Sam pushed herself up and straddled his face. He had the perfect view as she grasped the bars of the bed frame and started to ride his face.

Her juices began to pour out of her, covering his cheeks and chin. He lapped her up, thirsty for more. From her swollen clit to the pink folds to the sweetness of her opening, he adored every inch of her. *You need to remember how she tastes. And how she looks in this moment.*

Sam's hands were clamped tight around the frame. Her breasts bounced just above him. He reached up to caress them and she moaned at his touch. When she looked down at him, her smile was bright enough to burn into his memory, just as he'd wished.

"I used to imagine this," she said to him. He didn't remove his tongue from her.

The dim lighting from the lamp complemented her exquisitely. "I'm getting close," she whispered. He grasped her hips and held her down. When she came in his mouth, he drank her all in.

Exhausted, she fell beside him. "Your turn," she said as she reached for him.

"No," he said softly. "It's all about you tonight."

"You're in a generous mood," she said as she worried her lip. "But I want to."

"In the morning," he said gently. They were three of the hardest words he'd ever said.

She didn't push any farther, but turned her back toward him and spooned against his chest. Connor draped his arm over her and listened as her breathing turned steady in sleep.

He knew he should at least try to get some sleep before the flight tomorrow, but he just couldn't. Every moment was precious. Instead, he held her tight and watched as the sun rose over the water. At first, it was just a hint of dawn, but it slowly became evident that the day had fully arrived.

And he knew exactly what he had to do.

22

SAM

"Where's the other plane?" she asked as they boarded the smaller plane painted a midnight black.

"My father needed it, so we have the Piper Matrix," he said. "And don't worry, there aren't any 'servants' on board this one. Just us and the pilot."

She played with her hair and ignored the dig. Sam fell into one of the six seats, worn out from the so-called vacation. Muscles she didn't know she possessed hurt, and the ache between her legs was constant.

As they took off, she gazed out the window and watched their little slice of paradise disappear. In just a few hours, it would be back to the grind. A Tuesday morning in DC, normally a workday, but with the Fourth of July holiday she'd have an extra day to recover.

Sam looked at Connor next to her and had an idea. "The pilot's staying in the cockpit, right?" she asked.

"I certainly hope so." He flipped through the CNN app on his phone.

"Then how about we make use of the truly private flight?" she asked as she traced a hand along his thigh. Sam could see the bulge in his trousers had grown already.

"You sure?" he asked as he looked at her over the phone.

She felt a sting of uncertainty, but forged ahead. "Since when are you so shy?" she asked.

He tossed his phone on the seat across from him and pushed up the armrest that separated them. "I just don't want you to get too worn out," he growled into her ear as he pulled her on top of him.

She giggled as she straddled him. The short skirt and no underwear had been pre-planned—as had the tight shirt that zipped all the way open. Connor reclined the seat halfway while she unzipped him and stroked his shaft. He glanced at his watch.

"Are you timing me?" she asked. He reached for the zipper of her shirt and released her breasts slowly.

"Maybe," he said.

She guided him into her, slowly. Sam teased him at the tip, circling him in her wetness. He let out a huff of frustration and she lowered herself onto him. Connor went to grab her hips, control her like he liked to do, but she pushed his arms back. "You don't always get to be in charge," she said.

He obliged. As she fucked him at her own pace, every time he tried to reach for her she pushed his arms away. Sam wrapped her arms around his neck and pushed her breasts against his chest. Like this, fully in control, she could command when she would come—and as it turned out, him as well.

When he came inside her, it was the only time she let him grab onto her. He held her down, hard, onto him. She felt his release as it pumped into her, and it skyrocketed her to her own orgasm. His face was buried in her neck. It felt like an hour until he let her go.

She slid onto the seat beside him and pulled down her skirt. Connor didn't look at her, but simply buttoned his pants. "Restroom?" she asked, and he pointed behind them.

As she cleaned herself up in the little bathroom, using tissue to wipe between her legs, she couldn't help but feel like something was off. The sex had been fantastic, as always, but it was like he wasn't fully there.

She checked her hair in the mirror and finger combed it into submission. It didn't really matter anyway. Who was going to see her?

When she returned to her seat, he was engrossed in his phone once again. However, when he heard her approach, it seemed like he quickly switched from a different app back to the news.

"Since when are you such a news fiend?" she asked.

He shrugged. "I have alerts set up with my name, my father's, the company's—just seeing the publicity."

"Anything good?" she asked.

He held up an image of the two of them at one of last month's galas. It shocked her, seeing them on the local news like they were celebrities. They looked genuinely happy, like a real couple. The headline read, "Billionaire playboy and new Trezor COO settles down?"

"Looks legit," she told him.

"That's what I'm paying you for," he replied.

Sam left him to his phone for the remainder of the journey. It had to just be work, the mini-vacation being over, and all of that. He was moody, that was nothing new.

She stretched her limbs when the pilot announced the descent. A thick mass of clouds covered DC, regardless of it being summer. "I can't believe we're back to the real world," she said. The tired skidded along the runway.

"Sam, just so you know," he said. "What we had in Monaco? It was nice and all. But now that we're back, it has to stop. I'm sure you understand and know that—but just so we're clear."

She opened her mouth, but nothing came out. Sam was absolutely blown away. She wasn't sure what she'd thought or expected, but it certainly wasn't this. *And why not? Did you think he was in love with you?* Did this make her a prostitute? Was he paying extra for the "bonuses" in Monaco? She imagined herself throwing the extra cash in his face. Preferably with a full glass of alcohol to follow.

"Sam?" he asked. His eyes searched her face for some kind of reaction. "Look, I really need to get going. If you could just confirm that—"

"I get it," she said curtly. She reached for her bag and busied herself with a search for her keys and phone.

"And you intend to keep the terms of the contract?" he asked.

She realized she had some leverage here. She sighed, and knew she could get out of the contract at this point if she really wanted to. In fact, maybe that was what he wanted. Or did he expect her to ask for more money now? There was no way in hell that was happening.

"I keep my word. No matter what," she said. But she couldn't bring herself to look him in the eye. She was afraid she'd cry, or worse. The last thing she needed was to flip out on him.

Connor got up to leave. He didn't say a word.

She once again opened her mouth to say something. *Wasn't he at least going to give her a ride home? Sure, she'd taken an Uber to the airport, but she'd thought—fuck. She was a goddamned idiot.*

Sam powered up her phone and ordered an Uber. It was ten minutes away.

As she waited in the private area of Reagan, she couldn't believe it. She kept going over the weekend in her mind, looking for some kind of clue. *What did she miss? Did he really feel so little for her? Obviously. He made that quite clear.*

The Uber driver tried to make conversation on the way back. "I've never picked up anyone from that part of Reagan before!" the man with dreadlocks to his mid-back said. "You famous or something?"

"Or something," she said quietly.

He eyed her in the rearview and tried to make out who she might be. "I don't recognize your name," he said, and he held up the app. "You one of those millionaire YouTube beauty vloggers or something? You look like you could be."

"No," she said. "I just work for an asshole rich guy."

"Oh, I get you," he said. "I get some of those sometimes in my car."

When she walked into her home, it felt stale and foreign. Some of her houseplants had wilted already. Usually she'd ask a neighbor to water them, but Connor's request had come so fast—and early—she hadn't had time. "I'm sorry," she said to her plants as she watered them and situated the ones that liked it closer to the sun.

You just going to up and leave your life like that whenever he calls? But she'd meant what she said. She would fulfill this contract no matter what. It was a matter of pride at this point. And she'd just have to forget what had happened in Monaco.

She reached for her phone and texted Jenny. *Hey! Happy Fourth. Weird question, are you still on that dating app?*

Jenny replied immediately with a series of firework emojis. *Yes on the app. Why? You thinking of signing up?*

Was wondering if I could just check it out. Can I login as you?

Sure, haven't been on in awhile. Might be a ton of messages, just ignore them, she replied, along with the login information.

Sam downloaded the app. Her heart pounded as she logged in with Jenny's information. She hadn't been joking. There were over 200 unread messages and a slew of other notifications she didn't understand. Curious, she clicked on the fire icon.

Jenny had an impressive amount of matches. She'd matched with Connor just nine hours ago. Of course, it wasn't his real name, but Sam would know that photo anywhere. She'd taken it of him on the beach not even three days ago.

Sam slammed the phone down on the couch and tucked her knees under her chin. *I will not cry. I will not cry,* she told herself. *Is that what he was doing whenever we weren't fucking? Setting up hookups and dates for the minute he got back?*

She felt like the biggest fool. Worse, she hated herself for feeling anything for him at all. How could she be mad at him? He'd never pretended to be anything other than what he was.

Still, as she thought about the last four days and how over the moon she'd been, the tears started to fall. They were ugly, the kind that left her breathless.

Sam curled up onto the couch and let it all out. She wanted to hate him, but couldn't. This had all been her doing. She should have seen the signs.

When the doorbell rang, she quieted down and hid deeper into the couch. Heavy footsteps could be heard on the porch. It rang again. *If that's Connor, I don't even give a shit. I'm going to give him a piece of my mind.*

Her hurt had turned to rage, and she stomped toward the front door. She yanked it open to a scared-looking young kid holding a large package. "Oh, I was—are you… are you okay?" he asked.

"Fine," she snapped, and snatched the box from him.

"You're going fucking crazy," she told herself out loud. Sam opened the box and nearly laughed at herself. She'd forgotten all about it. It was a carton of bachelorette party items she'd ordered right before Monaco. She'd figured she might as well enjoy a raucous night out if she was going to fake a marriage.

She remembered how she'd looked forward to showing it to Connor, and how he'd surely get a kick out of it.

Sam dumped the contents into the garbage bin. She only felt a little bad about not donating the goods. But screw it, it felt too good.

23

CONNOR

It had been two days since they'd returned from Monaco, and he hadn't responded to her calls or texts. Even James was confused. "You have quite the light schedule this week," he'd remarked, and Connor had jumped on him.

"How is that any of your concern?" he'd snapped. James had simply raised a brow and gone about his business.

It had been hard enough telling Sam they couldn't continue. He'd spent the entirety of the flight trying to come up with the right words, but there were none. He'd settled on doing it hard and fast, but now he wasn't sure that had been the right approach.

She'd looked absolutely devastated. However, he'd already been committed. *Square your jaw and wipe the emotions off your face.* That was the advice his father had given him when he was in fifth grade and upset he hadn't made the basketball team.

He knew it had been a dick move to leave her at the airport. That hadn't been planned. But when he realized how heartbroken she was, and how much it hurt him, too, he just couldn't bear to be in a car with her and deal with the emotions.

It was an asshole thing to do, but probably better for both of them in the long run. Connor was sure he'd figure out his next move quickly, but he hadn't. Instead, he'd gone through the motions. He'd showed up to work promptly the next day, and James had pounced on him for details about Monaco. "Did she like the gowns? The swimsuits?" he'd asked eagerly.

"It's none of your business," Connor had snarled at him. James had jumped back the first time, but he'd adjusted quickly. For the past couple of days, he'd largely left Connor alone.

For once, he was grateful his father didn't give him any kind of actual work besides looking pretty and having drinks with clients. It gave him time to work on his plan.

When he saw her at the fundraiser at the Willard, he thought he'd be nervous—but he was relieved. Secretly, he thought she might not show up after the way he'd behaved. But she was there, right on time, and looked gorgeous. Clearly, James hadn't dropped the ball at all. He spotted her as she entered the lobby, and broke away from the group he was with. Without saying a word, he offered his arm and she took it.

"Hey," he said in a low voice. "You look great."

"Thank you," she said stiffly. She wore a Grace Kelly-inspired A-line dress with a sweetheart neckline and painstakingly intricate hand beading at the hem. She refused to make eye contact or her usual small talk with him.

When he touched the small of her back, he felt her cringe. *Shit, this isn't what I intended.*

A ridiculous part of him thought they could go back to how they used to be. The flirting and fun. *Why hadn't I just let that be enough? Why did I have to go and mess it all up?*

However, he couldn't accuse her of not doing her job. When it came time to make nice with the guests, she played her part beautifully. She talked, laughed, and smiled right on cue. It was just when it was the two of them that it all fell apart. When nobody was looking, she seemed miserable.

Finally, Connor left her alone when it wasn't required that they schmooze and look like the perfect couple. He needed to escape. He couldn't breathe around her. But he found that no relief came—he just turned more anxious.

Connor made his own rounds. He mingled and chatted with donors, but kept a watchful eye on her. Sam circled around to the women in the room. He watched her hug those whom she'd met before, or step back as she admired their shoes or dresses.

After awhile, he saw the Circle of Crones, as he called them, swoop in on her. They were ancient, even by his father's definition. The matrons of the DC donor crowd, they, or their husbands, were extraordinarily wealthy. When they gave, it was generous. However, to pry that money from their talons was a nearly impossible feat.

He could tell, even from across the room, that they'd started to grill her mercilessly. Connor felt a wave of protectiveness and made a dash across the ballroom to save her. He didn't care that he left his own conversation somewhat abruptly.

"Do you mind if I steal my bride-to-be for a moment?" he asked the old women as he plastered on a smile.

"By all means," one of the blue hairs said, and gestured them off with a flick of her gem-encrusted bony fingers.

Connor glanced down and expected a thankful smile from Sam. But all she gave him was a stony expression. *Damn. I'd started to expect that smile.*

He took her hand and pulled her to a quiet corner of the ballroom. "Sorry," he stammered. "I, um, I thought you could… you know, use some rescuing there—"

"Have you got your money's worth from me yet?" she asked coldly.

Connor pulled back. It felt like he'd been slapped. "What?"

"Well, it's clear you have a specific idea of how your 'fiancée' is supposed to behave. So, I'm just wondering, how am I doing?"

"Uh, good?" he asked. This was new territory and she clearly had the advantage. Though he didn't know how or what that meant. "Sam, I'm sorry," he said. "It's not you, it's me."

She gave a harsh laugh. "That line? Really? Wow, okay. Although, maybe you're right. Because it certainly is you."

"I know!" he said, then glanced around when he realized a couple of people had jumped at his voice. "I know, okay? I just… I don't like the idea of being too emotionally involved."

"Maybe you should have thought about that before taking me to Monaco and fucking me for four days," she whispered to him.

"I know," he agreed. "That was a mistake."

Her eyes widened.

"I don't mean that. You weren't a mistake. Jesus Christ. I mean, it was a mistake of me… doing that. It shouldn't have happened. Look, I don't—I've never liked the idea of being tied down."

"Oh, now I'm tying you down?" she asked. "You're the one who was engaged before. Not me. So, clearly, you do like being tied down. Just not with me."

His head spun. He couldn't keep track of what was happening, especially since her words seemed to make sense. "Listen, I want you to understand—"

"I understand perfectly," she said as she shot him a scathing look.

"I don't think you do," he said. "When I came up with this crazy idea of hiring you, I'll admit it was totally impulsive. That's not what I had in mind when I came to your work. I was pissed off, and it seemed like a good idea at the time, and I—"

"And you just thought you've bought everything else in life. Why not a fiancée? I'm a fucking moron," she said as she shook her head.

"Let me explain," he said. "And it's not you. I took advantage of the whole thing."

"Yeah," she agreed. "And I let you. Can I go now?" she asked, like she was asking permission from a parent. "I have a headache."

"Can I just try to get you to understand?"

"I read once that after twenty minutes, there's no point in talking or arguing anymore. Both parties have said all they can say at that particular time. So please, will you just let me go? You can make up whatever story you like to tell these people."

He sighed and looked around. Nobody watched them. It was like they didn't exist. "I'm not your keeper," he told her.

"Could have fooled me," she said and headed toward the door.

He watched her leave, and felt like an asshole. *How could you do something that would make her react like this?*

"Connor, where's the fiancée off to?" One of the donors, already drunk, wrapped his arm around Connor's shoulders and leaned into him.

"Women stuff," Connor said. "You know how it is."

"Actually, I don't," the donor said.

"Excuse me?"

"Gay. Remember?" he asked and wiggled his brows at Connor.

"Oh, yeah. Well, consider yourself lucky."

"Right," the donor said, suddenly pissed off. "Because it's *so hard* being a straight, white, rich male." He wandered off, and Connor berated himself. *How could I piss off one of the most promising donors?*

His touch had faded, and he could only blame himself. Sam made him crazy, and drove out all thoughts of the business from his mind. He couldn't stand that she was mad at him, but he couldn't come up with any way to win her over again.

He pulled out his phone and wondered if he should call her, or text her. But when he scrolled to her name, he just couldn't do it. Instead, he erased Sandra's name and typed in Sam. It was the least he could do.

Connor's notifications on the dating app had piled up. Simply to clear them, he clicked on it and went to "erase all." But he saw that a familiar-looking girl had matched with him, and viewed him recently.

"Jenny_fromthe_Ward" didn't look particularly like his type. Although that night in Monaco, he'd swiped right like a maniac without even looking. He clicked on her profile and went through the handful of pictures. She was kind of cute, petite with a severe black bob. "I'm an event manager," she'd written.

Event manager? *Shit.* He realized exactly who she was. What were the odds of Sam's coworker getting matched with him on the app? Well, pretty high, actually. Everyone was on it. And he'd never not matched with anyone before.

What if Jenny told Sam? The girl didn't seem particularly confident or outgoing. Was she a gossip? How close were they exactly? And what if Sam figured out he'd matched with this girl while they were in Monaco?

You're overreacting, he told himself. *There's no way that will happen.*

Connor clicked off the app quickly, as if that would do anything to erase what he'd done. Again he went to Sam's name in his contacts, but he couldn't think of what to say. Maybe he should just give her more time to cool down. Do something now, and it might blow everything up.

"What are you doing over here like a wallflower?" His dad came out of nowhere, as per usual. "Go out there and mingle. Where's Sam?"

"She was just here," he said. "And I've mingled them to death."

"Yeah? Carlos didn't seem too happy just now," his father said, as he nodded toward the donor Connor had just insulted.

He sighed. "He'll get over it."

"I certainly hope so. The last thing we need is one of the most influential young donors in the city claiming Trezor is homophobic, racist, or both."

Yeah. I'm *the one who's going to give us that reputation.*

24

SAM

Sam bit into another of Aunt Mary's famous soft oatmeal cookies and moaned. "I don't know how you do it," she told the older woman.

"Cold ghee, not butter," she said simply, and placed down two cold glasses of cashew milk for her and Ellie.

"I'm so glad you never sold this house," Sam told her. "I have fond college memories of waking up here on Sunday mornings!"

"And me pretending I didn't know you girls were hungover as all get out," she said. "Ain't no amount of cheap cocktails a few cookies can't fix."

"I wish a hangover was the worst of it," Sam said.

Ellie held her hand across the table. "It'll be okay," she said. "You have my full attention for the next few days. Especially with Henry going all James Bond with his US Marshals mission and everything," she said with a smile.

Sam let out a deep sigh. "Thanks," she said. "To both of you. But this is good. It helps. I just—God, I just need to get away from my life for awhile."

"You know," Ellie said gently, "you don't have to keep up this charade. Why don't you let me look at the contract? I'm sure there's something in there—"

Sam made a face and cut her off. "Oh, I'm going to finish out the month, and then I'm quitting. You can bet on that. I'm tired of his bullshit."

"Language," Aunt Mary said.

"Sorry," she said, ashamed. "That's how crazy he makes me! You see? Ugh, I wish I hadn't gotten mixed up in this whole mess."

"That's what you get when something sounds too good to be true," Aunt Mary said as she sat down with them. "How much did you say he was paying you again?"

"Um, a lot," Sam said. It embarrassed her to say the amount out loud. She'd cut the real number in half when she'd told Ellie, and Ellie had still flipped out.

"Well, money isn't more important than your sanity," Ellie said. She pulled her thick red hair up into a ponytail.

"I don't get this whole 'arrangement' thing," Aunt Mary said. "Are you allowed to date other people during it? Is he?"

"As far as I know," Sam said. "I can tell you for certain *he* is, that's a fact."

"Well, then if you don't mind the advice of an old woman, I suggest you do just that."

"What do you mean?" Sam asked. Already, Ellie had perked up.

"Go out tonight. Meet some fellows. Have fun, for goodness' sake. You're young and beautiful!" Aunt Mary said. "And you," she said to Ellie. "You be a good wingwoman while our Henry's gone. You deserve to go out, too. I know he can be a bit of a stick in the mud."

Ellie blushed and looked away. "Aunt Mary, I didn't exactly bring any clubbing clothes with me. That wasn't what I was expecting when we decided I'd stay the week with you."

"You girls and your excuses. I'm sure Sam has something you can borrow."

Sam locked eyes with Ellie, who arched an eyebrow at her. "Why not?" Ellie said. "Just because I'm coupled up doesn't mean I can't be one hell of a wingwoman."

"That's the spirit!" Aunt Mary said. "Just make sure you take a taxi. And don't worry. I won't wait up." She began to clear the plates, and they jumped up to help.

"Where should we go?" Ellie asked her as they scrubbed the plates in the farmhouse sink.

"Ugh, somewhere that *doesn't* remind me of him, please," Sam said. "Wait, I have an idea." She grabbed the newspaper from the counter and flipped to the arts section. "Here," she said, and pointed to a half-page ad. "A huge barbecue and beer festival going on today and tomorrow.

There's no way he'd be caught dead there." However, in the back of her mind, she remembered that killer smokehouse he'd taken her to. But that had just been a one-off oddity, for sure.

Ellie wrinkled her nose. "It doesn't exactly have a club type of vibe…"

"No, but look! There are horses available. Wouldn't it be awesome to go on a ride again, like we used to? And afterward, some barbeque. Some beer. Some cowboys…"

Ellie laughed. "Sounds like you have it all figured out," she said. "I'm in. When's it start? Three? Let's do it."

They raced up the stairs to get ready in Henry's old room.

"Good girl, Gypsy," Sam cooed as she patted the rich brown mare with a bright blaze of white on her nose.

"I have to say, this is the first time I've been armed with a squirt gun on a ride," Ellie said beside her as she examined the fluorescent green gun.

Sam shrugged. "Who knows? These kinds of events are always managed by hipsters."

Whether it was a slow amble or a trot, being in the saddle wore on her thighs and groin. It annoyed her that even out on a ranch, she was reminded of Connor. Sam couldn't wait until all traces of that shitstorm in Monaco were out of her system.

After two hours on the trail, they were helped off the horses by muscled, middle-aged farmhands. "You lovely ladies have a good time," one of them said as he eyed Ellie in her skintight jeans.

They dug into the Louisiana-style baby back ribs, creamy coleslaw and buttery cornbread with gusto. "I don't know what it is about riding," Sam said. "But it gets my appetite going like no other. I'd weigh three hundred pounds if I ever lived on a ranch."

"Yeah, right," Ellie said with a laugh. "And it would all go to your boobs and butt, I'm sure!"

She swatted at her as she wiped her hands on the wet towelettes that came with their paper plates. Sam swallowed the last of her beer and shook the bottle. "I could go for something stronger," she said.

Ellie pointed to the barn. "They have whiskey and moonshine back there," she said. "I saw a sign."

"You want to?" Sam asked with a grin.

Ellie laughed. "Sure. As soon as you wipe that sauce off your cheek."

They ordered doubles of Jack Daniels on the rocks and walked around the side of the barn. "I can't believe you did that!" she squealed to Sam.

"I didn't do anything! They did! I just asked if they'd fill our guns with the moonshine. They didn't have to. Watch out!"

Ellie barely avoided a sun-baked cow pie. "I wish I'd brought my cowboy boots to Aunt Mary's," she grumbled.

Sam rolled her eyes. "You look perfectly fine!" she said.

"Hey, look," Ellie said, but she didn't need to tell Sam. A group of five guys around thirty years old were tipsy while they made full use of the water guns.

"They never grow up," Sam said with a laugh. But she had to admit they were cute. It was in a private area, far from the festival grounds. One of the guys had already stripped his plaid button-up off and had it draped over the stable fencing.

"Looks like we have a crowd," the blond guy said as he caught sight of them. "Sorry, ladies, no voyeurs allowed. You either join in, or you mosey along."

"Mosey?" Sam asked. "Sounds like you've been on this farm too long."

She saw two of the guys nudge each other in back as they sized her and Ellie up. They wore wide grins that matched. "Those are the rules," the blond said as he approached them.

Ellie giggled and deferred to Sam. It had been a long time since Ellie was single, but Sam had this. She looked at his chest, which was either bare or clean-shaven. He wasn't nearly as bulked up as Connor, but he wasn't slight like the models either. It was an all-American type of build, and in its foreignness to her it was attractive.

Sam looked him in the eye, raised her gun and sprayed him lightly. "Who's the voyeur now?" she asked.

He laughed and backed away. "Holy shit, that's not water."

"Moonshine," she said with a smile.

He raised his own gun and sprayed her white shirt. She crossed her arms over her chest in protest. "Hey! Not fair, you didn't have a shirt on."

"Nobody's making you keep yours on," he teased her. The boys descended on them and aimed for their chest. Both her and Ellie's tight white tank tops were instantly soaked through. *Here's to wearing cute, bright lace bras under Hanes tank tops,* she thought to herself.

"Give me some of that," a boy with long black hair said to Ellie, and forced her to squeeze some of the moonshine into his mouth.

"Totally not fair," Ellie said. "You're lucky we were nice and didn't drown you in cheap liquor."

"What can we say? We have a thing for nice girls," one of the guys said.

"So, what are you two up to now?" the blond asked. "This will be shutting down soon. I mean, unless you're staying for the campfire events and stuff."

"Nah, I think we've had enough," Sam said.

"Cool. So, you want to hang out? Or…"

Ellie looked at her. It was all up to Sam. "Sure!" she said.

"Great, any ideas? We're not from around here, so we're kind of playing it by ear."

"How about Kabin?" Sam asked. She couldn't stop the words from coming out. It had to be the whiskey, that was it. But she felt emboldened and strong. *Who gives a fuck?*

Ellie shot her a look.

"Uh, sure," the guy said. "Never heard of it. Here, let me put my number in your phone and you can text me the address."

Even as she typed in the address to the club, she started to have doubts. Sam brushed them aside and took another swallow from the whiskey.

"Looks fancy," the guy said as he looked up the place.

"You'll be fine as long as you have a button-up," she said. "How about we meet there at ten? We need to go home and change. You know, change out of our wet t-shirt outfits and all," she said with a wink.

He smiled at her, and she recognized the look. He thought he'd score tonight. *Maybe he will,* Sam thought.

"Sam," Ellie hissed as they headed for their Uber. "That's where you ran into Connor last time! Are you sure this is a good idea?"

Sam knew Connor would probably be there, but she didn't care. That was the point, she realized. "It's fine!" she reassured Ellie. "It'll be fun. Besides, what are the odds of him being there tonight anyway?"

"I don't know," Ellie said pointedly. "Do you?"

Sam sighed. *What was the big deal if she wanted to make Connor jealous? It's not like he owned the freaking club. She could go where she wanted, with who she wanted.*

"Just be careful," Ellie said. "This was supposed to be a fun night out. Remember? I said I'd be your wingman, but I don't know what I'm getting myself into with—"

"Relax," Sam said as she wove her arm through Ellie's. "What's the worst that could happen?"

25

CONNOR

He stepped out of the shower, grateful to wash the workout sweat from his body. Ever since he'd left Sam on that plane, he'd doubled down at the gym. It was the only place and the only way he could focus on anything besides her.

Connor vaguely remembered Arnold Schwarzenegger talking about his Mr. Universe days. Working out was likened to a blackout. He'd said it didn't even really click when he got a call that his father had died. He'd just gone right back to his reps.

That's what Connor hoped for.

However, it was mostly quantity and not quality. He barely slept, and insomnia wasn't the best accoutrement to gym sessions. He couldn't lift as much as he used to, and his reps weren't as high. He powered through them, but mostly it was cardio. When he looked at the time and realized he'd somehow lost an hour on the treadmill, it felt like a gift.

Connor rubbed the towel over his wet hair. His phone buzzed. *Isn't this your girl?* It was from Jay, who had attached a grainy shot of what appeared to be Sam. She was bent over while a young guy with blond hair dry-humped her on the dance floor.

Automatically, his fists clenched when he saw the hands on her hips. *Where are you?* he asked Jay.

Connor was absolutely livid as he got dressed. *Just because the contract doesn't stipulate we can't date other people, that gives her no right to rub it in.*

Sam knew damn good and well he frequented that club. As did his friends. What did she think was going to happen? He pulled on his Tom Ford jeans and rolled up the sleeves of his Burberry shirt. He'd show her what it meant to cross him.

Connor threw the keys at the valet and marched to the front of the line. There were protests from those who'd been standing there for hours, but he shook hands with the familiar bouncer, handed him a hundred-dollar bill, and stepped inside.

"Connor!" Jay spotted him instantly.

"Hey," he said, and they pounded each other on the back. "Where is—"

"She's over there," Jay said, and pointed at the dance floor.

He saw her in a barely-there turquoise dress. Now, she was with another guy who had thick black hair to his shoulders. Connor stormed through the crowd, which parted easily for him.

Connor grabbed Sam's forearm, and she looked up in shock. "Come on," he said, and pulled her.

"Hey man, what are you doing?" the guy asked.

"Don't get in the middle of this," he warned him.

"Connor!" she said, as she tried to yank her arm free.

"It doesn't look like she wants to go with —"

Before the guy could finish, Connor released Sam's arm and punched him squarely in the jaw. There were gasps around them and a wide circle cleared.

"Fuck, man, what's your problem?" the guy asked. He cupped his jaw and stared at him.

"Connor, you're gonna have to go." The bouncer was suddenly at his side.

"Sorry man, I'm going," he said. "She's coming with me."

He took Sam by the elbow and urged her along. Surprisingly, she obliged, though she trailed slightly behind him.

Connor directed her to an alley around the corner where they could still hear the sounds from the club. "What the hell was that?" she asked.

"You tell me! I get this photo of you basically fucking some guy on the dance floor —"

"Not from me, you didn't!" she said. "It's not my fault if you have your little spies set up all over the city."

"Spies? Hardly. You know damn well my friends and I come here. How do you think that looks? Just because you can technically do what you like off the clock, that doesn't mean you can sabotage what we've built in the process."

"Me?" she asked. She stepped directly in front of him and he could smell the sweet cocktail on her breath. "I'm not the one who sabotaged anything! I was minding my own business, finally having a fun night out for once, and you crashed in here like a goddamned caveman. I'm not the one who created a scene. That was all you."

He was enraged with her, but at the same time she was irresistible to him. "You fucking drive me crazy, you know that?"

She rolled her eyes, but before she could speak, his hands were on her waist and he'd closed the distance between them. Sam's lips parted easily, and his tongue found hers. He walked them back, just three steps, and pushed her against the brick wall.

Her hands were on his chest, beneath his jacket. He'd missed this, this hunger she had for him that he could never quite tame.

Connor hadn't seen anyone else in the alley, but now he wouldn't have even cared. He reached underneath her short dress and found a skimpy lace thong. It tore easily in his hands, and he cast it aside.

His mouth was on her neck while he sucked and nibbled. Sam's breath was heavy in his ear. He slipped a finger between her folds. She already gushed with want, and let out a low moan at his touch.

Connor went back to her mouth and kissed her deeply. He pulled her breasts from her dress. Either the chill of the night, his touch, or both had her nipples hard in an instant. With ease, as if she weighed nothing, he hoisted her up around his waist and she wrapped her legs around him.

He leveraged her against the wall and sucked her nipples. When she pushed her wetness against the bulge in his jeans, he sucked harder until she let out a cry.

Carefully, he put her back down and turned her around. With her back to him, and her dark hair cascading down her back, he peeled up the unbelievably tight bottom of her skirt to reveal her ass.

Connor gripped her hips and yanked her back a couple of steps. Forced to bend over at a sharp angle, her palms pressed against the wall, he slapped her ass. It made an incredible echo into the night.

"Look at me," he told her, and she gazed at him over her shoulder. Connor slid two fingers into her and she squeezed her eyes shut as she let out a gasp.

He fucked her with his hand and began to increase the speed. Still, he held her steady with his other hand—not that she would move even if she could.

When he felt her start to get close, he released her waist and bent down. Connor kissed one of her full cheeks before he bit lightly. As he slid his fingers out of her and began to circle her clit, he flicked his tongue across her rim. Sam flinched, just barely, but she didn't move. And she didn't try to stop him.

He wouldn't go any farther than that, not now. He tasted the most secret part of her and worked her clit faster.

Connor could feel her wetness start to flood. It trickled down her thighs. Occasionally, he would leave her rim to lap up the trails along her thighs.

"Did you miss this?" he asked her before he dove his tongue into her opening.

"Yes," she whispered.

"I said, did you miss this?" he asked again, and pressed harder into her clit.

"Yes," she said, louder into the night.

"Are you going to come for me?" he asked, even as her clit was swollen more than he'd ever seen.

"I don't—"

"Come for me," he demanded. He moved back to her rim, and squeezed her ass apart with his hands. He could hear her as she panted. Connor took a finger back to her clit while he slid a thumb inside her. Sam started to command her own rhythm as she rocked back and forth against his face.

When he dipped his head to taste more of her, he could see that she played with her breasts. "Good girl," he told her, and she moaned at his words.

Connor brought her closer to orgasm. He hit her G-spot and worked his tongue expertly. His erection pushed painfully against his jeans, but he didn't care. All he wanted was to make her come.

"Are you going to come for me?" he asked her again.

"I'm—now—"

He buried his face deep into her, and felt the rock of her orgasm as it shook her entire body. She cried out, but he didn't let her go. It wasn't until he'd drank every trace of her orgasm that he stood up, squeezed her ass again, and turned her around. He didn't even bother to wipe his face. He wanted her to cover him, evidence of what he could make her do.

She was weak on her stilettos, her face and chest flushed. He ran a hand across her bare chest, and squeezed a nipple between his thumb and finger. There were still the slightest hints of his hickeys on her chest. He'd been a goddamned idiot to treat her the way he had.

He looked down at her swollen clit, emerged from the hood. He could fuck her all day. Her wetness was evident, spread along her mound and the fronts of her thighs.

Sam panted lightly, still in the afterglow of the orgasm.

Connor went to unbuckle his jeans, and her eyes moved from his groin back to his eyes. She smiled. Finally.

His erection nearly hurt, he needed her so badly. Connor reached out and ran his finger across her lips while he pulled his length out. He left a trace of her come, and she licked it away.

Sam bit her lip and pulled him toward her. She maintained eye contact, and it was impossible to look anywhere but deep in that green abyss. He went to kiss her, but she ducked away—shy, like a schoolgirl. Instead, she lowered into a crouch, his cock inches from her lips. He looked to either side of the alley, but saw nothing.

Below him, Sam looked like a goddess. *What did I do to deserve this?* She looked up at him and gave him another one of those smiles he'd been so desperate for the past few days.

Connor closed his eyes, grasped his base, and waited to feel her lips on him. He could still remember the magic of her mouth. How it had felt when she'd taken him into the back of her throat. How she had licked the precum from his tip like it was the best thing she'd ever tasted.

"This has to stop," she said, her voice like ice. He opened his eyes, and she stood once more, her mouth against his ear. She'd thrown his words from the plane right back at him.

Sam had tucked her breasts back in her dress and pulled down the hem.

She turned and stormed down the alley, somehow balancing on those cobblestone streets even in dangerously high heels.

Connor was left holding his dick alone in the alley, his mouth open and the taste of her all over his face.

26

SAM

*S*am chewed on the pencil at her desk and stared at her computer screen. She'd been that way for an hour, but for some reason this client email was impossible to write.

Scratch that, she knew the reason. She couldn't concentrate on a damn thing after what had happened in that alley.

She sighed, and instead sent the file to her boss that had been requested that morning. Immediately, a message popped up. *This isn't what I asked for???* Mrs. Whiteworth replied.

Shit. She'd messed up the simplest of tasks all day. Sam could still smell him on her. But it wasn't just that—no matter how many times she ran over the event in her head, she just couldn't figure him out. Was he just jealous? Perhaps. Horny? Definitely.

Still, she thought there was more to it than that. She'd dealt with jealous, horny men before. None of them had that fire in their eyes that he'd held the other night.

It was obvious he liked her. That much was evident when he nearly dragged her out of the club Tarzan-style. Sure, she'd egged him on. Ellie had called her out on that. She hadn't known what he would do, but she hadn't expected what had happened.

And now she was more attracted to him than ever.

Idiot! she thought to herself. Sam couldn't help how she felt, but she knew how he treated her was wrong. Misogyny nearly sweated out his pores at times. How he treated all women was wrong. There were certainly hints that maybe he was more like his dad than he seemed. *No, he's not. You're wrong.*

Sam breathed out deeply and put her head on her desk.

"Taking a lie down, are we?" Mrs. Whiteworth asked. Sam's head snapped up. She hadn't heard the woman walk in. She walked like a cat, always on the prowl and silent.

"I'm sorry," she said. Her entire body coursed with embarrassment. She scrambled for excuses, but came up with nothing. An apology would have to be enough.

"Sam," the older woman said as she walked close to the desk. She crossed her arms over her chest and looked down at her. "Are you alright?"

That simple question nearly brought Sam to tears. She would not cry at work. How weak was she? "I'm fine," she said, and forced a smile. "Really. I'm sorry about that wrong attachment, I'll send it over right now."

"I'm not concerned with the file at the moment," the woman said. She smiled kindly at her. "I didn't come all the way over here to make pleasantries. I asked if you're alright."

"I don't know," Sam said slowly. She realized it was the most honest thing she'd said in awhile. The time with Ellie and Aunt Mary had been good. They soothed her. But it had also just fed her wild need to lure Connor in. With Mrs. Whiteworth, she'd been caught at her most vulnerable.

"You can talk to me, you know," the woman said. "I know I don't always seem like the *warmest* person in the world. And I'm not HR, and I'm not your mom, but it's clear you're going through some things."

"I… I won't let it impact my work again," Sam promised with new resolve.

"Sweetheart, you can't do it all," she said. "Trust me. What are you, twenty-six? Twenty-five?"

Sam nodded. Twenty-five years old and mooning over some boy like she was sixteen. How did she let it come to this?

"It's a beast of an age," Mrs. Whiteworth said. "I was twenty-five once. I worked in the catering department for a company that no longer exists, but served every political gala in the city."

Sam looked at her with a new perspective. She couldn't imagine the regal woman in a black apron with platters of food.

"Don't look at me like that," the woman said with a laugh. "I *did*, really. And I was quite good at it. I wanted to be a chef, like Julia Child. Well, not like her, but you know what I mean."

"A chef," Sam repeated. *What do I want to be?* It had been so long since she'd pondered it. She knew she wasn't cut out for a great career in event management, that was for sure.

"And I was crazy in love. Or lust. Thought I was, at least," Mrs. Whiteworth said. "The kind where I was happy to throw everything away for it."

Sam blushed. *Was I that easy to read?* "What… what happened?" she asked.

Mrs. Whiteworth sat down in one of the guest chairs. "He was the son of a very influential politician at the time. If I told you his surname, you'd probably be able to guess. I met him when I was helping to cater one of those godawful snoozefests."

She cocked her head and looked at the elegant woman. Sam couldn't imagine her being anything but poised. And able to get anything she liked.

"But," Mrs. Whiteworth continued with a sigh. "It didn't work out. As you can see," she said, and waved her bare ring hand at Sam.

"Was it unrequited?" Sam asked. She nearly laughed at the word herself.

"Unrequited? No, not entirely," Mrs. Whiteworth said with a smile. "I like to think not. We carried on in secret. For nearly a year, in fact. He worried that being with me would mar his family's reputation. His budding political career."

Sam looked at her lap. It all sounded too familiar. Although Connor had never told her that outright. She'd never asked or looked into Sandra's background. *What did Sandra have that she didn't? The right upbringing? The right education? What's wrong with me?*

Mrs. Whiteworth leaned toward her. "If he doesn't see what a catch you are, he's a moron," she told her.

"How did you know?" she asked. *And how much do you know? Did she know Connor was a client?*

"It's obvious, I'm afraid," Mrs. Whiteworth said. She held up a finger to her lips. "Don't worry. I don't think the rest of the office knows. It takes age, and experience to be able to see it. Plus, your generation is so obsessed with their own lives, they barely notice others exist."

Sam's face burned. She was part of that generation, of course. And Mrs. Whiteworth was right. When was the last time she'd taken a genuine interest in anyone's well-being at work? When was the last time she'd noticed anything about them unless it had to do with her, too? She couldn't help but think of poor Jenny. She'd swooped in on her when she'd thought Connor was hot on that first day, and she'd been unfairly angry at her with the whole dating app thing—even though she'd never approached her about it.

She didn't know a damn thing about Jenny, and they'd started at nearly the same time.

"I had no idea." It was all she could think of to say.

"Don't blame yourself," Mrs. Whiteworth said. "You're young. I know you're probably tired of hearing that at this point in your life, but it's true. You have no idea how young, or how much is ahead of you. I know it feels like whatever you're going through right now is too heavy to carry. Trust me, it isn't. You're a strong woman."

Sam blushed at the unexpected compliment. She wanted to look away; the woman's eyes were almost too intense. But she forced herself to hold the gaze. "Why do you think that?" she asked. She wanted to take it back. It sounded too much like she was fishing for compliments.

"You think I'd hire anything else?" Mrs. Whiteworth asked.

She went over the roster of employees in her head. Mrs. Whiteworth was right. There were elements to all of them that were impressive. How else would this agency have so quickly become the powerhouse in the industry it was?

"Just remember," Mrs. Whiteworth said as she stood up. "You can talk to me."

"Mrs. Whiteworth?" she asked as the woman was halfway to the door. She turned in her flawlessly tailored Chanel and looked at Sam. "Why event management?" she asked.

The woman laughed. "Turns out I was shit in the kitchen," she said. "I went to culinary school when I was forty. Or tried, at least. This is the next closest thing. As it turns out, I never wanted to be a chef. What I wanted was to throw one hell of a party."

Sam smiled. The woman was forty before she even gave what she really wanted a chance. There was time. There was time to decide. "And the boy?" she asked. "What happened to him?"

Mrs. Whiteworth sighed. "I wish I could tell you I don't know," she said. "That he disappeared into the great wild, that all I carry of him are romantic notions of what he could be doing. Who he could be. But this is a small town at its core," she said. "All I can tell you is he followed, diligently, in his family's footsteps. Although, do you want to know something?" she asked.

Sam leaned forward, the promise of a secret way too tempting to pass up. "What?"

"He got bald and fat before he was thirty-five," she said with a conspiratorial grin. "My torch for him went out long ago. That doesn't happen with real love, does it? Believe me, you're not too old to still be confusing lust for love."

Sam sat back and let that soak in. *Was she right? Is that all this was?*

The glass doors to her office swung shut in silence.

Sam leaned back in her white leather chair and wondered about the self-imposed deadline. It was just a few days away. When she'd said she'd just finish up the month, she'd meant it. She didn't care that she hadn't told Connor. Who was he to deserve a notice, anyway?

That's it, she thought to herself. *You have until the end of the month. Either you get him to see things your way, or let him go.*

That was easier said than done. Sam searched Connor's name and a plethora of images popped up of the two of them together. A few local bloggers guessed at their potential wedding date. Some completely made up how the two of them met. *Journalism at its finest,* she thought.

Still, she had to admit they looked more than good together. They looked right.

She knew she shouldn't do it as soon as her fingers started to type the name. Sandra Brewer. It took her a few minutes to narrow down the search—but there she was.

Moderately pretty and largely unassuming. Sam was surprised. It wasn't the airhead hot blonde she'd expected.

The girl had gone to Vassar, worked at an NGO, and was from a town in Connecticut she'd never heard of. She seemed moderately well-off and educated, but not leaps and bounds "better" than Sam in any regard. *Why her and not me?*

Sam stared at a photo of Sandra until her image had to be permanently burned into her brain. She just couldn't figure it out.

Why did she get the real engagement?

CONNOR

Connor couldn't remember the last time he'd been this nervous. With every ring of the phone, he prayed that she wouldn't answer. Not that he wanted to leave a voicemail, either, though.

"What?" Sam said for an answer.

"Hi," he said. "Um, I know it's last minute, but my family is having an overnight retreat—"

She gave a mean laugh. "And let me guess, I'm expected to accompany you."

"Well, yeah."

"What kind of family has a 'retreat' anyway?" she asked.

"Apparently mine," he said. "I know it sounds ridiculous, and it's usually in the autumn, but due to a ton of stuff, it got changed last minute to tomorrow."

She sighed. "And what exactly does such a 'retreat' entail?"

"You'll be somewhat happy to know it's simply an overnight stay at The Cottage."

"Really?" she asked. Sam seemed to warm to the idea that it was nearby, only required a thirty minute drive, and The Cottage was known for the saltwater pools, massages and pampering, and not much else.

"So, can you do it?" he asked.

"I don't have much of a choice, do I? Just one thing."

"What's that?"

"I drive there myself. I don't care what excuse you tell your family. I don't want to spend a second longer with you than I have to."

"Agreed," he said.

"*That* Sam of yours is certainly a dedicated career woman!" his mother said as she nursed her Arnold Palmer.

Sean rolled his eyes while he worked on his second gin and tonic of the morning.

"Quite impressive, quite impressive," his father agreed. "Of course, I expect you've talked to her about lightening up her 'duties' after the wedding? You know what such demands can do on a girl who's expecting—"

"Yeah, yeah," Connor said. He checked his phone again, and as if Sam had been waiting, a text popped up.

Five min away, she said.

"She's almost here," Connor told his family. He stood up and brushed the croissant crumbs from his lap. "I'm going to go meet her."

"Perfect timing," his mother said. "I'm sure the two of you will love the couple's massage I booked for you."

"Oh, I'm sure," Connor said. It took all his power to force the sarcasm out of his voice.

Sam was just walking up the steps to the resort with her camel tote bag when he walked onto the patio. She looked beautiful as always in wide-legged white linen pants and a bright pink silky top. "Here," he began as he reached for the tote. "Let me —"

"I can handle a bag, Connor," she hissed as she tucked her sunglasses into her tote. In a second, her expression changed completely. A warm smile spread across her face. For a moment, he thought maybe she'd somehow forgiven him, though he couldn't fathom why.

"Hello, dear!" his mother cooed from behind him. She rushed past Connor and embraced Sam in her arms. "It's so lovely to see you. And don't you look beautiful!"

"So do you," Sam said sweetly. "I just love that dress."

"Vintage," his mom told her quietly, as if it were a secret. "Connor's father hates how I adore these 'old clothes,' but men don't understand much, do they?"

"No, they certainly don't," Sam agreed. She looked at Connor pointedly.

She gave a twinkling laugh. "I'll let you two get settled in your room. I've booked a couple's massage for you that starts in, oh, an hour. You know," his mother said as she hooked arms with Sam, "I'd booked one for his father and I, too, but the man absolutely refuses. Says he doesn't want some stranger fondling him."

Connor thought he saw Sam stiffen slightly at the mention of a couple's massage. If she had, she'd recovered nicely. She told his mother it sounded wonderful.

"Here we are," Connor said as he opened the door to their suite.

"It's just one bed," Sam said.

"Yeah, well, my parents booked the rooms. I couldn't exactly ask them for bunk beds."

She made a face at him and tossed her bag on the chaise. "I'll sleep on the couch," she said.

"Don't be so dramatic. Do you need to change or anything? Before the massage?"

"Oh, I don't think so," she said. "Who do I have to impress? I mean, we won't be seeing your parents for a couple of hours, will we?"

In the dimly lit massage room, the two middle-aged women waited for them, warmed oils at the ready along with hot stones. "Please go ahead and remove everything, except your underwear if you'd like, and get under the sheet," one of the women said. "Face down. We'll be back in just a moment."

Sam turned her back to him as she undressed. It was maddening. He wanted to tell her not to bother, that it wasn't anything he hadn't seen before. But he still found himself getting aroused as he stole peeks at her bare back. He felt an erection shift when he took in the fullness of her ass in that satin underwear. *Stop it,* he thought to himself. *That's exactly what you need in a massage room is a raging hardon.*

She didn't look at him at all as she slipped under the white sheet and nestled her face into the massage table opening. Connor took the moment to give her a long, hard look. He couldn't see much anymore, but it might be the last time he could gaze at her unabashedly.

When he heard a knock at the door, he quickly got under his own covers. The two women went to work as the New Age music swelled in the room. "How long have you two been engaged?" the brunette who worked on Connor asked.

"Engaged? Not long now," he said. "But we dated for quite a bit before that."

"Ah, yes, I think I saw a photo of you two in the pap—"

The woman stopped herself before she could reveal that she knew who he was. It was uncouth to act like you read the gossip column at such a posh place. He heard Sam sigh contentedly as the blonde who hovered over her hit a sweet spot. "Have you ever had a couple's massage together before?" the woman asked her.

"No," Sam said quietly.

"It's very romantic," the woman said. "I recommend all couples get one at least every few months. It can work wonders, especially when stress at home or work is high.

It's a good reminder of simply being together and pampering yourselves. You know?

Connor nearly laughed. It felt good, but if this woman thought a massage was all it was going to take to fix their problems, she was crazy.

After the massage, he had to admit he felt loose and calm all over. Even Sam walked back to their room in a more languid way than he'd ever seen. She didn't even barge ahead of him like she tended to do these days. He felt a buzz in his pocket and pulled his phone out. "Fuck," he said.

She looked at him curiously.

"I thought—damnit. The whole family's coming after all."

"What do you mean the whole family?"

"The extended family. Two uncles, an aunt, and all their kids and grandkids."

"*What?*"

"I'm sorry. My mother had told me they couldn't make it given the last-minute change of plans."

Sam sighed as they stepped into their suite. Someone, he guessed his mother, had ordered red flower petals to be sprinkled across the bed with a bottle of chilled champagne on the nightstand. "Did you—"

"It wasn't me," he said quickly.

"You're really testing me," she said. Sam pulled a dress out of her bag and shut the bathroom door hard behind her.

. . .

$\mathcal{C}$onnor took Sam on the requisite rounds as the whole family gathered for pre-dinner cocktails. Even he could barely remember some of the names, especially of the kids, and was wildly impressed at Sam's ability to charm. She cooed at and held all the babies, connected with his cousins, and won over even his gruff uncle Bernard with ease.

As he watched her immerse herself in his family, he could easily see her there for good. It was natural. A few times he caught his father watching her, but what the hell? Let him. He knew that even in the state they were in right now, Sam would never do anything.

Dinner was largely uneventful. There were toasts, and quite a few were directed at them and their impending marriage. "May we perhaps set a date once and for all this weekend," his father had said to a round of cheers. Sam smiled broadly, as if that was her greatest wish, too.

"Everyone's drunk," he whispered to her by nine o'clock.

Sam nearly laughed, or so he thought. The two glasses of champagne had softened her.

"Want to make our escape?"

She nodded, took the last swallow of the bubbly, and accepted his hand when he offered it. She didn't let go, not even when they were far out of sight.

In their room, she threw herself onto the bed. A flurry of red rose petals exploded from around her. Connor took a white pillow and tossed it on the couch to start making his bed.

"No," she said. "It's fine." Sam patted the bed. "There's plenty of room for both of us. What difference does one more night make?"

What does she mean by that?

Connor went to the bed cautiously. When he lay down, she turned on her side to face him and tucked a pillow under her cheek. "I hope I did okay tonight. Because —"

He cut her off. Whatever she was going to say next, he didn't want to hear. "You did great." *As always.*

She hadn't changed out of her bright orange dress. It had hitched up close to the apex of her hip. He could see her cleavage easily through the peephole neckline. He reached out and touched her arm. "Sam —"

She closed the distance between them. As soon as he felt her lips on his, all bets were off. His body responded like he'd been starved, and he pulled her against him. His hands squeezed her waist and tested the swell of her hips. He needed to be certain she was real.

Their tongues met, and she bit his lower lip gently. Connor caressed one of her breasts through the thin summer material. She responded with a leg over his.

It was insane, how he simultaneously felt like he already knew every inch of her and how she was still a mystery every time. Connor wiped a stray lock of her hair from her cheek and held her jaw in his hand.

He needed her immensely. As he reached under her dress to pull down her underwear, she moaned in pleasure — and that seemed to break the spell. Sam's eyes shot open as she froze. She looked at him like she'd just woken up and found him assaulting her.

She pushed back, eyes big. "What…"

Fuck. He didn't know what to say or what to do. Frustrated and angry at her, at himself, he got up silently and threw himself on the couch. Somehow, on that little velvet settee with his back to her, he forced sleep upon himself after what seemed like hours.

The last thing he remembered was listening to her running the shower in the bathroom.

2 8

SAM

When Sam woke up, Connor was nowhere to be found. She eased her head up from the pillow and looked around the suite. Flower petals were everywhere, and the expensive bottle of champagne's label was peeling in the bucket of melted ice. She spotted a note left on the nightstand.

Out golfing. That's all it said.

She let out a breath. *Good.* After what had happened last night, and her stupid mistake thanks to the champagne, she was grateful that he was gone.

Her hair was still slightly damp from the late night shower. Somehow, she'd managed to get a good night's sleep. Sam blamed the champagne and the sheer exhaustion of putting on a show for a room full of strangers all night.

She pulled on a pair of light denim shorts and a loose floral blouse that fell off of one shoulder. As she slid on her gold strappy sandals, she gazed into the mirror. It was one of those rare occasions when her naturally wavy hair had behaved perfectly. It looked like she'd spent hours at the salon. With just a swipe of rosy lip gloss and a touch of mascara, she grabbed her sunglasses and headed to the breakfast area.

Sam didn't recognize anyone, and glanced at her phone. Eight o'clock. She supposed it might still be a little early for some people.

The waiter rushed to her little table on the patio. Sam ordered a latte and an English scone. The thick white linen tablecloth and fresh flower arrangement was, admittedly, lovely. She tried to take it all in while she could. Checkout was in the afternoon. When her latte arrived alongside the little currant scone, she smiled at the idyll heart made with the milk.

"A beautiful girl should never eat breakfast alone."

Sam jumped at the voice and looked up. It was Connor's father, looking surprisingly disheveled without his usual suit and tie. Instead, he wore long gray shorts and a short-sleeved Tommy Bahama-style shirt. It looked fake, like he was an actor playing a role. And not very well.

"Mr. Harris! You startled me," she said.

She couldn't read his eyes behind the mirrored sunglasses, but had the suspicion he angled to see down her shirt. He made no reply.

"Um, would you like to join me?" she asked. Suddenly, she wished Connor was there. Anyone except his sleazy father.

"Connor hasn't accompanied you?" he asked. He looked around the empty restaurant.

"No, he, uh… he scheduled a morning golf game. With some of his cousins, I think."

"Huh," his father said as he sat down uncomfortably close to her. "I thought that boy hated golf. Well," he said as he removed his sunglasses. "Maybe his tastes have improved as he's matured." When he said it, he looked blatantly at her thighs.

She wanted desperately to make her shorts longer, but resisted the urge to tug at them. The waiter appeared with a black coffee and slice of frosted lemon bread. He hadn't even had to ask. Instead, she toyed with the massive engagement ring she'd at least had the sense to put on that morning.

His father watched her, appraised her, and bit into the sweet slice of bread. She watched crumbs as they gathered at the corners of his mouth and fell into his lap. "You're different than what Connor's slinked around with before," he said.

"Oh?" She daintily sipped her latte and tried not to make any more eye contact than was necessary.

"Oh, yes. Trust me, I know. Particularly that last one. *Sandra.*"

She looked at him and saw the game in his eyes. *Did he know? Should she play dumb, correct him? Act like he thought she got her name wrong? What the hell was he on about?*

"You're a special girl," he said, and leaned forward. He was dangerously close. Suddenly she felt his hand on her leg. It was close to her knee, perhaps not technically out of line. Still, she opted to cross her legs the other way, away from him, rather than actually remove his hand. He laughed.

"Okay," she said. She wanted to buy time as she figured out his angle.

"I have a proposition for you," he said, and her heart sank. She'd heard those words before. They sounded eerie coming from his father just a few weeks after Connor had spoken them. *He's going to ask me to break up with Connor for money.* A part of her was thankful, though she wasn't sure how she should respond.

As she began to tear through options in her head, his hand creeped higher on her thigh. Now it was in dangerous territory. "We both know you're marrying Connor for his money. But that's a very big commitment just for a payday. Don't you think?"

Her eyes widened. *How did he know? Did he know the whole thing?* She was frozen, unable to swat his hand away. "I—"

"Let's cut to the chase. Yes, perhaps it's feasible you'd get a pretty generous cut if you stayed married to him for, oh, I don't know, seven years or more? But that's the prime of your life. Even if you got away with affairs, got lucky and he got swallowed up in nonstop work, you're still throwing your life away for a check."

She swallowed. *He didn't know.* He just thought she was an average gold digger. Part of her was relieved, and part of her raged with anger. *A gold digger? Maybe that was what she was after all.* "I don't—"

"Sweetie, let me make this really easy on you. You've gotten me hard every time I've seen you since day one. I have a separate suite here booked nobody knows about. What do you say you, me, and an hour in the honeymoon suite for twenty thousand dollars? Then you walk away for good. How does that sound?"

"Twenty thousand dollars?" It was the same initial price Connor had offered her, and she couldn't help but echo it. But she saw his smile and realized he thought that was an agreement. "No! I—"

"Alright, alright," he chuckled. "You drive a hard bargain! Let's make it twenty-five. How many times are you going to be offered that kind of change for an hour of your services? And, I must say, I'm being generous," he said. "It's not usually my thing to pick up my son's sloppy seconds. What do you say?"

Her face burned a bright red. Finally, her body started to work with her brain again and she pushed his hand off her thigh. "I say fuck you," she said with a hiss and stood up.

As she walked off, she heard him laugh behind her. "Honey, that was exactly what I was trying to do!"

Connor jumped when she walked into the suite. He must have thought she'd busied herself for the entire morning. "Hey!" he said. "My, uh, golf game got finished early—"

"Your dad just propositioned me for sex," she said coldly.

"What?"

"You fucking heard me. Twenty — no, twenty-*five* thousand dollars for an hour with him. That price sound familiar?"

Connor's face turned to stone. "Where is he?"

"Last I knew, feeling me up on the breakfast patio."

Connor blew past her and started down the hall. *Shit. What had she done?* "Connor! Connor, wait," she said and started after him. *What the hell did you expect?*

By the time she caught up with him, he had already reached his father. The son of a bitch had stayed to finish his lemon slice. Sam could make out a few words, but not everything. His father stood, and she realized Connor had a good four inches on him. But his father's paunch made him seem somehow larger. It also put a buffer between the two of them.

"…just sample the new family goods," his father finished as she approached.

Connor decked him and Sam gasped. Bright red blood sprayed across the white tablecloth. She heard waitstaff as they ran around behind her. His father wiped his face, saw the blood and laughed. "You just wrote yourself out of a job. And out of your inheritance," he said.

"That's fucking fine by me," he said.

"Connor! What happened? What did you —"

His mother appeared in the doorway and rushed to his father's side.

"Come on," Connor said to Sam, and grabbed her by the elbow. She couldn't have resisted if she wanted to. She wanted nothing more than to get out of that room.

He took her around back to the covered porch which was reserved for special events. It was empty this time of day with the chairs stacked on the tables. Connor's entire body shook, and she put a hand on his back. "I'm sorry," she said.

"You're sorry? For what, exactly?" he asked. She'd never heard his voice like this before.

"For—"

"Not taking him up on the offer?" he asked.

It felt like he'd slapped her. "What? Don't be crazy," she said.

"You know what? Maybe you're right. Maybe I am crazy," he said. "This whole thing, this whole fucked up charade, was insane. And you know what's even crazier? That you went along with it."

"What?"

He laughed, and just a tiny part of him looked like his father in that moment. "Of course I'm fucked up in the head. Look at my goddamned family. But you? Some raving client comes into your office and you agree to be his fake fiancée why? For the money? Because he gets your panties wet? Both? Who's the fucked up one now, huh?"

She backed away from him. This wasn't what she'd expected. Worse, he was right. Of course he was right.

She was just as messed up as he was. The tears started to come, and she couldn't stop them.

"Don't give me that," he snapped. "Turn on the water-works to get what you want. I'm immune to that bullshit. My mom pulled it my entire life."

"I can't help it," she said. It was hard to get any words out.

"Forget it," he said. "And forget you." He turned and walked at a fast clip directly into the woods. She could make out some kind of trail, but it looked abandoned at best.

"Connor!" she yelled after him, but he'd disappeared into the green.

Sam took the stairs to their room to avoid any run-ins. As she stuffed her belongings into her bag, she realized she couldn't fix him. He was who he was.

Tears streamed down her face, and she pulled the ring from her finger. She left it on the dresser and pulled out a piece of paper to leave a note. But found she had nothing left to say.

2 9

———

SAM

It had been three weeks since that nightmare at The Cottage and Sam still hadn't completely shaken what had happened off her. She dragged ass at work, and knew it. Connor had called and texted a few times, but she'd ignored him. She hadn't listened to the voicemails and deleted the texts without reading them. Simply seeing that one of them started with, *Sorry about…* was enough to make her sick.

However, she started to think that it was more than disgust and heartbreak. She felt like hell. She took her temperature daily, and it felt like she had the flu but her temperature was just barely raised.

"You look like crap," Jenny told her when she finally forced herself to come into the office. It was Friday, but she'd taken the entire week off. The least she could do was prove she wasn't off on some tropical vacation.

Sam had already sweated through her light blouse by the time she collapsed into her desk chair. "I feel like crap," she told Jenny.

Her coworker hovered in her door. "Do you want me to get you some water? Maybe—"

Sam couldn't help it. She leaned over and vomited into her trash bin.

"Oh my God…"

Jenny covered her mouth, and Sam was just grateful she hadn't been able to gag anything down that morning except half a grapefruit. "Sorry," she said. "I… I don't feel good."

"I think maybe you should go back home," Jenny said.

"I agree." Mrs. Whiteworth stood behind Jenny.

Jesus. Sam shone with embarrassment. Had her boss seen her vomit? She'd never live that down.

"We don't want you spreading whatever this is around the office," Mrs. Whiteworth said. "I'm guessing you're sick? Not hungover, right?"

Sam could barely face the woman, but when she looked at her she saw a glimmer of kindness in her eyes. Mrs. Whiteworth put on her own charade daily. She couldn't let the whole office know she was soft underneath that hard exterior. "No, ma'am," she said. "I… I think I have the flu."

"Go home. Rest over the weekend. If you feel up to it on Monday, come in. Otherwise, I'm sure you have a few more sick days remaining." Mrs. Whiteworth turned on her heels and walked away. Jenny widened her eyes at Sam.

When Sam got home, she grabbed her oversized crocheted blanket and curled up on the couch with a cup of chicken broth. Mindless daytime television, specifically the Bravo network, was sure to distract her.

Her phone buzzed on the couch. *If this is Connor again, I swear to God —*

But it was Ellie on Facetime. "Hey," Sam said as she answered. She wished Ellie would just use the regular call feature, but it would look weird if she didn't answer.

"Hey! I wasn't sure if you'd answer, but I thought this was your lunch break. Where, um, where are you?" Ellie asked. "Are you at home?" She could see her friend as she tried to make out Sam's background.

"Yeah, I'm a little sick," Sam said. "Just going to binge some trashy reality TV and ride it out."

"Sick, huh?" Ellie said suspiciously. "You're never sick. And you never miss work."

Sam sighed. She should have known Ellie wouldn't accept such an excuse. "I know," she said. "I don't know what's wrong with me! I feel like I have the flu, but every time I take my temperature it's just barely elevated. I think the thermometer's broken."

"You feel like you have the flu?" Ellie asked. "How so? Just hot? Or …"

"Hot, tired. No, exhausted, actually. And I—I threw up at work. Like, in front of my boss."

"Oh, God," Ellie said. "I'm sorry. But, um, Sam? I don't think you're sick…"

"What do you mean?" she asked. She sipped the broth from her faded university mug.

"Babe, it sounds like… you're pregnant," Ellie said.

"Pregnant?" Sam laughed. "That's ridiculous! How could I be—"

Oh, fuck. I'm a goddamned idiot. All those times. We hadn't used protection any of those times. Why is this just now occurring to me?

"Sam?" Ellie asked.

"Oh, God. Oh, God, shit, Ellie. What have I done?"

"It's okay! Hey, it's okay. You don't know anything for certain right now. You just need to take a test to be certain that's all. I mean, I barely know what I'm talking about."

"No," Sam said. "You do." She remembered Ellie's ectopic pregnancy. She hadn't told many people—in fact, Sam was one of just two people outside Ellie or Henry's family who knew. "How did you… how did you know? When you were pregnant?"

Ellie sighed. "I took a test," she said. "But, honestly? I also just kind of knew."

"Yeah," Sam said. "I know what you mean." The thought hadn't occurred to her before, but as soon as Ellie said it she knew she might be right. "Where are you?" she asked Ellie.

"Getting on a plane at LAX in three hours," Ellie said. "I'm coming. Don't worry. Go to Aunt Mary's for now, I'll meet you there. There's a direct flight, I'll be there by early evening. Actually," Ellie leaned closer to the phone and whispered. "I think I have some pregnancy tests still stashed away at Aunt Mary's, too. Check in the bottom center drawer of Henry's old bathroom."

"Okay," Sam said. She'd started to sniffle. "Those don't, like, go bad or anything, do they?"

Ellie laughed. "I'm not an expert. But probably not within a year, no."

"Good," Sam said. "Because the last thing I need right now is to go into a store and buy one of those things."

"I'll call Aunt Mary and tell her what's going on," Ellie said.

"Thanks, E," Sam said. "I don't know what I'd do without you." It was true. And it was a great comfort to have that kind of support in her life.

"Don't be weird," Ellie said. "Love you, see you soon."

Sam was on autopilot as she drove toward Aunt Mary's. She hadn't even changed out of the yoga pants and thin t-shirt she'd put on when she got home. Braless and in flip-flops, she drove like hell toward what she thought of as her last sanctuary.

"Sam, dear," Aunt Mary said as she opened the door and held her tight. "I made you some cookies."

Sam laughed into the older woman's hair. Somehow, yes, cookies sounded like they could fix everything. "Oatmeal raisin?" she asked.

"Snickerdoodle," she said.

Sam wiped the last of the tears from the corners of her eyes. "How much… how much did Ellie tell you?" she asked.

"I think quite a bit, dear," Aunt Mary said. "Don't you worry. Everything will be okay. No matter what."

Sam followed her into the tiny kitchen and sat down at the round wooden table. Cookies before pregnancy tests. That seemed the way to go. She bit into the warm sweetness and closed her eyes. Instantly, she was brought back to one of her fondest memories. Ellie had just started to date Henry, and they'd spend the night here on the weekends — hungover from the bars while Aunt Mary cooked them greasy blue-collar breakfasts.

"I wish I could take it all back," she said aloud.

"Don't ever wish that," Aunt Mary said. "Come what may, it's all meant to be."

"I don't know," Sam said. She stood with her plate, but Aunt Mary blocked her way to the sink.

"I'll deal with that," she said. "You just go on upstairs."

Ellie had emailed her the flight details. Sam took her time on the stairs. It felt like she was on a ship's plank and had no idea what waited for her at the end.

Ellie had been right. There was an unopened box of pregnancy tests at the back of the bathroom cupboard.

She pulled it out and looked at the instructions. *Stupid. You pee on the stick. Everyone knows that.* Still, she wanted to know exactly what to hope for. This test was easy. Yes for pregnant, No for not pregnant. Nobody could mess this up.

Sam pulled down her yoga pants and hovered over the toilet. *What if I can't pee? What if I get an error? What if it's wrong, no matter what it said?*

She shouldn't have worried. A trickle of urine released, like her body knew exactly what was needed. Sam sat the test on the counter, pulled down the toilet lid, and waited. She watched the clock on her phone and refused to even peek at the test until the full three minutes were up.

I just knew, that's what Ellie had said. She got that, completely. It felt like she wasn't alone, like there was someone else with her. *That's what pregnancy feels like.*

When her clock showed 4:12, she stood up and looked at the test. There was no way to get it wrong. *Yes*, the test read.

Sam crumpled onto the floor. She missed the toilet and it banged painfully into her backside. She didn't care, she was thankful for a second of distraction. Fresh tears began to pour out of her. *What the hell am I going to do with a baby?*

"Sam?" Aunt Mary appeared in the doorway. "Oh, honey. It's positive?"

She couldn't speak, she just nodded, and buried her face in her hands.

"Come here, come here," Aunt Mary said. The old woman surprised her with her strength as she pulled her to her feet. She led her into the living room and Sam collapsed onto the couch.

She cried, unrestrained, in Aunt Mary's lap. Sam felt like a child again. Aunt Mary petted her back and smoothed her hair. "I know, I know," she told her.

What did she know? She didn't know anything! Sam swallowed her bitterness, refused to let her fear and anger leak out onto this kind woman. "What… what am I going to do?" she sputtered. "I didn't want any of this. I didn't plan any of this."

But you did! What did you think was going to happen? How many times did you let him come in you—beg him to come in you? She ran over all the times she'd been with Connor, all the stupidity, and it brought on a fresh river of tears.

"It's going to be okay," Aunt Mary said. "I promise. You just let it all out for now."

She listened to the comforting words and did as Aunt Mary said. When all the tears had dried up, she felt lighter. Like her bones were hollow. Still, she stayed with her head in the woman's lap all the way until Ellie walked through the door.

30

———

CONNOR

"What's wrong with you, man?" Chase asked as Connor scratched yet again at the billiards table.

"Who are you, my mother?" Connor snarled. Chase looked at him in surprise. "Sorry, just off my game today."

"Testy, testy," Jay said.

Connor took a deep breath and avoided the bait. It had been a month since the shitshow at The Cottage, and he hadn't heard a word from Sam. Not for his lack of trying, and not that he blamed her. He couldn't believe how his father had acted—actually, that was wrong. His father had been his usual self. What Connor couldn't believe was how he'd reacted.

He kept going over their last conversation in his head. She'd confided in him, that was all. *She wasn't Sandra.* He didn't know why that realization was so hard to sink in. Instead of just protecting her, like he should have done, he took the opportunity to rail at his father and then turned around and blamed her, too.

He was so goddamned blinded by his past, he didn't stop for even a second to think about her. She never would have done that to him. It was no surprise that his father had propositioned her. Actually, Connor was surprised it had taken his father so long.

Connor knew that Sam would never take his father up on anything. But in that moment, all he'd seen was red.

It had taken him an hour to cool down in the woods. At first, he'd stomped around like mad. Scared rabbits had darted out of bushes. But slowly, he'd calmed down. Nature had hugged him close, and it had soothed him. The crunch of his shoes on the ground and the twittering of birds had eventually had a calming effect on him.

By the time he'd circled back around to The Cottage, he'd made up his mind. He'd make an apology, a genuine one, and smooth everything over. He was madly in love with her. He'd known it for quite some time. Why had he been so stubborn about it?

Connor had broken out into a smile when he saw the stately white resort come into view. He'd bounded up the steps and raced to their suite. The first thing he'd noticed was all her belongings were gone. Then he'd seen the ring on the dresser with a blank piece of paper beside it.

It was a small gesture, but it had gutted him to the core. He knew it was over for good. Of course he'd have James get all the money to her, but he didn't give a damn about any of that. He just wanted her.

He'd stopped trying to reach her after six voicemails and countless texts. Connor could tell she'd read none of them. She probably deleted them as soon as they came in.

"Fuck," he said loudly as one of the solids, for the other team, went neatly into a pocket.

He stood up and saw Jay and Chase give each other a look. "Why don't you just call her?" Chase asked.

Connor was startled. *Was he that obvious? Why didn't they assume it was about work or something?* It's not like he'd told them his father had fired him from his lofty figurehead position.

"I don't know what you're talking about," he said as he chalked his cue stick. There was already a thick layer of blue on the tip.

"Dude, come on," Jay said. "We're tired of your moody ass. It's been a month and you're not letting up."

"Can we just get back to the game?" he asked.

"We'd love to! If you could remember how to play," Chase said.

Connor sighed. They were right. He'd thought of nothing else for the past month but Sam. She'd been right all along. That line he'd given her about not wanting to be tied down was childish. It was immature and needlessly hurtful. Besides, he'd been engaged before—to her, it must have looked like an obvious jab.

He wandered to the bar and pulled out his phone. It went directly to her voicemail. *Damn.* Connor downed the last of his lukewarm beer. "Hey, guys," he said as he walked back to the billiards table, "I'm gonna head out."

"Yeah?" Chase asked. "Early day tomorrow?"

"Something like that," he said.

He was almost home when his phone lit up with a text from her. *I need to see you. Your place*, she said. His heart started to pound.

Finally. He'd get a chance to apologize and everything could be made right. It was all he wanted. Her, that was all he wanted. *Be there in ten*, he replied.

When he pulled up, she was on the porch steps. His headlights hit her, and his heart lifted. She looked amazing in tight jeans and a flowy peasant blouse. Without having to try, she always looked perfect. But there was a look of worry on her face.

"Sam," he said, and bolted out of his car. "I'm sorry, I—"

"Don't," she said as she held up a hand. "I need to get this out." She took a deep breath. "I want you to know, I don't expect anything from you. Financially, emotionally or otherwise. But I still think you deserve to know."

It was obviously a pre-planned speech, and he forced himself to be quiet. It was the least he could do for her.

"You and I, I know it was just a business arrangement. And I don't blame you any more than I do myself for this. But telling you is the right thing to do—"

He went rigid. "What are you trying to say?" he asked. Though he knew, deep down. He just needed to hear her say the words.

The color drained out of her face. "I'm pregnant."

He was stunned. Just two words to change your life forever. "You're… I'm…"

"If you're going to ask if it's yours, yes," she said.

He nearly laughed. "I know that," he said. "I don't doubt it—"

"I just, I thought you should know. And I'm going to have it, so don't try to talk me out of it. Or buy me off or whatever. And if you want to be involved in some way, that's totally your call, but if not that's okay, too—"

He kissed her into silence. *God, she tasted good.* It felt like home, natural and easy. He got hints of those multi-layered fruity gum pieces she loved, and her own sweet scent.

When they broke apart, he pressed his forehead against hers. "I'm sorry," he said. "I wish I could say more, but that's the heart of it. I'm sorry for all the things I've done wrong, for all the assumptions I made. You didn't deserve any of it."

She looked at him with tears in her eyes.

"Do you, do you think you can forgive me?"

"Forgive you, yes," she said. "But I… I don't know if I want you back."

His breath hitched. Connor's head hung heavy. "I know I was wrong," he said. "About so many things, countless things. And this isn't an excuse, but—your past gets you. You know? My father, growing up in his shadow. There were times, with you, where I saw parts of him come out in me and I hated it."

"You're not like your father," she said.

"And then there was Sandra. My ex. She—God, I guess she fucked me up worse than I thought. It didn't help that I tried to make you just slide neatly into her place. And my dad, he bought her and then tried to pull the same stunt with you—"

"None of that matters," she said simply. He realized she was right.

"I know," he said. "I'm sorry."

"Connor," she said as she put her hands on his shoulders. "I… look, if you ever so much as think about treating me like that again, even a whiff of it, I'm gone. Do you understand?"

A smile stretched across his face. *She would take him back. He'd get one last chance.* "I get it," he said.

"This isn't a game anymore," she said. "Game's over."

He held her chin in his hands and looked into her eyes. "I know," he said. "You know, I've… I've never even thought about being a father."

She bit her lip and looked down. He traced a hand along her stomach. It felt just as smooth and taut as ever, but he swore he could feel the baby just centimeters from his fingers. A miracle had happened.

"Well, I never thought about being a mother," she said. "Not anytime soon, anyway."

"Plans are for suckers," he said, and she laughed.

"I, you know, I think I know when it happened," she said.

"Really? How could you possibly narrow it down?" he teased her.

"Call it a mother's instinct," she said. "But I know. Just like I knew I was pregnant without having to see the test. Monaco."

"Really?" he asked. "I mean, that makes sense. We didn't really do anything else during that time—"

She punched him lightly on the arm. Connor pulled her into his arms and carried her inside. She giggled and batted at his back. "Put me down!" she said. "You're carrying precious cargo."

"You've always been precious cargo," he told her as he set her gently on his bed. "It's just that it's been doubled now."

"So you're not mad?" she asked. He was shocked, but saw the honesty in her eyes. *How could she possibly think he'd be mad?*

"Of course not!" he said. "I'm surprised, but happy. Isn't that funny? I'm happy."

She took his hand. "That's not funny at all," she said. "I'm glad. I'm happy, too."

He kissed her and they stretched out on his bed. When he kissed her from her ripe lips to down past her throat, he lingered at her stomach and held his head against her warm skin. "What do you hear?" she asked quietly.

"Your heartbeat," he told her. "It's fast."

She giggled. "Can you blame me?"

As he pressed his ear softly against her stomach, he tried to imagine all the magic that had happened below the surface. They'd done this. They'd made this. *I promise, I'll be a good father to you,* he said to himself. Connor was certain the baby could read his mind. *You won't know anything like what I did.*

"Hey," Sam said softly. "Are you falling asleep down there?"

"Sorry," he said, and kissed his way back up. "Just having a moment."

31

SAM

*S*am was over the moon. She'd spent the last few days in bed with Connor, and god it had felt good.

It was the same, yet deliciously different, in Connor's bed. She'd been more than shocked at how happy he was with the news. When he'd undressed her just now, he'd been overly gentle.

"I'm not going to break," she'd teased him.

In response, he'd bitten her neck and made her squeal. He'd whipped off her shorts and pulled her to a seated position. When he'd lifted her arms overhead with her blouse, he'd paused for a moment. Her wrists had been bound in his hand, and she couldn't see anything with the shirt over her eyes.

But her mouth was free. She felt his lips on hers, and the width of his tongue as it traced her own. Naked and exposed, the cool breeze from his open window played across her breasts.

"Connor," she said, and struggled against his hold.

She could hear the smile in his voice. "Patience," he said.

She smiled in response, into his kiss, while he kept her arms overhead. Sam could only sense his next moves. He pulled at her lip with his teeth and wandered his mouth to her earlobe. Connor sucked at her neck while his other hand traced circles at her areolas.

Slowly, his hand moved downward. He hovered at her stomach, but kept going. Sam spread her legs eagerly, desperate to have him. He barely glanced across her clit, but it brought a shiver down her body.

"You're always so wet," he said, as if in disbelief. She pressed against his finger as he swept them through her folds. Bringing the warm juices to her mouth, he spread her excitement across her lips and kissed her deeply. Finally, he finished removing her blouse.

She opened her eyes as he lowered her down. Connor knelt between her legs, pulled off his own shirt and unbuttoned his jeans. Sam pulled eagerly at his thighs in an attempt to get him closer.

"Eager, are we?" he asked. He slid his length along her clit and let her wetness act as the only lubricant.

Sam arched her back. She wanted him inside her, needed him inside her. "Connor," she started to say, but he obliged her and slid in deep. She gasped out, and he grabbed hold of her hips.

He brought her to orgasm quickly and used his thumb to manipulate her clit while he fucked her slowly. Sam squeezed at her nipples, and watched his gorgeous face as he gazed down at her. "You're beautiful," he told her right as she came.

He wasn't far behind. As soon as the first wave hit her, he gave a small cry and emptied himself into her. Sam's nails dug into his thighs. "Stay," she said softly. She wanted to feel his hardness inside her all the way until the end.

Spent, he stretched onto his back beside her. "Thought of any names yet?" he asked.

She turned on her side and faced him. "I've barely had enough time to even process it as a reality."

"How many people know?" he asked.

"Just two. Well, three now, including you."

"Who are the other two?" he asked.

"Ellie and Aunt Mary," she said with a shrug. "And that wasn't even planned. Ellie just happened to Facetime me at the right time, and she knew. There's no tricking that girl. It didn't help that…"

"That what?"

"Well, she'd been pregnant once, too. Lost it though."

"I'm sorry," Connor said. "But she's young. Are they going to try again?"

She smiled at him. "I don't know. They weren't exactly trying the first time. I still can't believe it! There's no way I even would have guessed I'd be the first of my friends to have a baby."

"I can only imagine what my mother will say," he said with a shake of his head. "She'll want to start planning a shower immediately."

"It's way too soon to tell anyone," she said softly. Sam traced patterns along his chest.

"It is?"

"Let's at least wait until after the first trimester."

"Dang," he said. "No names, no baby shower, I thought women got all baby crazy."

"Give me time," she said with a grin. "I just need to get there. I'm probably still in as much shock as you! But don't worry, I've already been researching weird symptoms and things like that. I'm sure I'll be suitably crazy by the time the baby gets here."

"Let me talk to her?" he asked, suddenly. Connor looked eager and excited like she'd never seen him before.

"Her? Her who?"

He gestured to her stomach.

"What makes you think it's a girl?" she asked.

"I don't know. I didn't really think about it, it just sounded right."

She had to agree. "What are you going to say?" she asked with a laugh as he lowered himself to her stomach.

"It's a secret," he said. She thought he was joking, but he spoke so softly to her stomach she barely made out any words. He faced away from her, and his voice created the tiniest of winds across her stomach. No matter what he said, the love in his voice was palpable.

"Are you going to be one of those people who plays Beethoven against my stomach for the next eight months?" she asked when he'd finished.

"Is that supposed to help?" he asked.

She rolled her eyes. "So… what now? I have to be honest. I kind of thought I'd just say my piece and be out of here. I didn't expect this."

"You underestimated me," he said with a wink. "Don't worry, it's not your fault. It's mine."

"You still didn't answer me," she said.

"Well, I don't know how much you've heard. Technically, I was laid off. Though, it was really more of a combination of quitting and being fired. After I sucker punched my dad at The Cottage, he wasn't exactly keen on having me at the office."

"Oh," she said softly.

"It's alright. I was going to quit anyway. And really, he couldn't exactly just fire the COO like that. It required board approval and cutting through a ton of red tape. I think it was best for everyone. I got a pretty sweet severance package, though."

"Connor, I'm so happy for you," she said. Sam propped herself up on an elbow. "I know how miserable you were there."

"Yeah," he said. "It's… I don't know. Scary in ways, I guess. But I'm going to set out on my own. I don't know if it will be in security, but there's got to be something SEAL training has prepared me for."

"There's always event management," she said with a laugh.

"Don't tempt me."

"I don't know," she said. "I feel like we're in the same boat. Not that I can compare my job to yours in the least. On so many levels. But I'm just floating by, you know? I certainly don't love my job."

"Maybe we can figure something out together," he said.

"What do you mean?"

"Who knows. A few weeks ago I never would have fathomed being where we are now. And now, I can't imagine it any other way. What do you say? The three of us against the world."

She cradled her stomach and looked at him. "I couldn't see it any other way," she said. She let out a breath. "What does your mom say about all this, though? I like her, even though she lets your dad use her as a doormat. I can't imagine what she's going through."

"She's tougher than she looks," he said. "But, like I said, she's going to absolutely flip over the baby. I know, I know, it's a secret for a little bit longer. But trust me, that's going to be her whole world when she finds out."

"I haven't even thought about telling my mom yet," Sam said. "Or the people at work! God, they're going to flip out."

"In a good way?" he asked.

She shrugged. "Ellie and Aunt Mary are already over the moon. I was so terrified when I found out for certain. You know? And it was just a couple of days ago, but now I can't figure out why."

"Well, you and I do tend to do things out of order when it comes to us," he said.

"What do you mean?"

"Well, we got engaged first. Broke up next. Baby after that."

"Broke up?" she asked. "How can you break up with someone you've paid to be your faux fiancée?"

"You'd be surprised what I can do," he said and raised her brows at her.

She laughed. "No. Nothing you do surprises me anymore. I've got your number, mister."

"Oh yeah?" he asked. "How about this then?"

He reached toward his nightstand and pulled out the familiar engagement box.

"You didn't!" she said. It was a beautiful ring, but there was a piece of her that was saddened. In some ways, it would always remind her of how they started—the ugly and the good. Plus, she'd look ridiculous with that beast on her in almost every situation.

"You're right, I didn't," he said. He looked sheepish. "Sorry, but I couldn't bear to take any excess that reeked of my father's money."

"Huh?" she asked, and he opened the box.

Inside was a light pink gem surrounded by a small cluster of diamonds. Sam caught her breath. It was absolutely breathtaking, and completely her. "Connor, it's—"

"It's a sapphire," he said. "Believe it or not. The most well-known color is blue, but they actually come in a variety of hues."

"Wait, are you? Are you asking me?"

He dropped to the carpet beside the bed on one knee. "I never told you the real reason I always thought sapphires would be the engagement ring I'd buy," he said. "In the thirteenth century, engagement rings were introduced. They were usually sapphire, because it was believed the gem would change color if worn by an untruthful person."

Sam blushed.

"But that's not what this is about. I have no doubts of your honesty, just as you shouldn't have any doubts of my love for you. And, believe it or not, this ring I bought completely with my own money. From my military account. I know it's not as impressive as the other—"

"It's perfect," she said.

"So, is that a yes?"

"I don't know," she teased. "You didn't really ask, now did you?"

He smiled up at her. "Are you going to marry me or not?"

Sam kissed him, putting all her emotion into it, and let the kiss answer for her. She was in this thing, for the long haul. Forever.

32

There's a little bit more of Ryan and Poppy, just waiting for you! Get this bonus story FREE — right now — when you sign up for Vivian's mailing list! Head to https://bookhip.com/TNGVNT_for more info.

Thank you for reading His Fiancé To Keep! I know if you liked this book, you will LOVE Elijah and Meredith's story, HIS LOVELY VIRGIN! Now on Kindle Unlimited!

A rich politician chasing the power of the highest office in the land. A naive young reporter assigned to follow him on the campaign trail. A sizzling secret she whispers in his ear about how he could be her first.

He's a billionaire with obscenely good looks, on the campaign trail to become the next president. She's a sweet little blonde reporter who is much too young for him. The moment she whispers her secret - that she's never been with anyone before - he's hooked.

Despite his ruthless pursuit of the presidency, he can't resist her. She's a temptation he can't ignore, even though she's dangerous; she jeopardizes everything he's worked for. But when she pulls him in for a kiss, he knows he can't resist, and he'll stop at nothing to make her his.

Their night of passion is everything he imagined and more. He can't shake the feeling that he's falling for her. He's wealthy, lavish, and has an empire at his fingertips, but he wants her to be his more than anything.

Jealousy rears its ugly head as he sees her talking to other men on the campaign bus. He knows he needs to make her his for good. He'll stop at nothing to keep her by his side, even if it means risking his political career.

One thing is clear: Meredith is his, and he'll stop at nothing to keep her that way. Their love is decadent, steamy, and all-consuming, and he knows he'll do anything to make sure she stays in his arms.

One-click HIS LOVELY VIRGIN!

ABOUT VIVIAN WOOD

Vivian likes to write about troubled, deeply flawed alpha males and the fiery, kick-ass women who bring them to their knees.

Vivian's lasting motto in romance is a quote from a favorite song: "Soulmates never die."

Be sure to join her email list to keep up with all the awesome giveaways, author videos, ARC opportunities, and more!

VIVIAN'S WORKS

MARRIED AT MIDNIGHT SERIES
FORBIDDEN BILLIONAIRE ROMANCE
DEAL WITH THE DEVIL
WED TO THE DEVIL

Vow to the he Devil

Ruined castle series
Forbidden Billionaire Romance
The Scottish Billionaire
The Beast
The nanny
The caress

Broken Slipper series
Forbidden Billionaire Romance
The Patron
The Dancer
The Embrace
Possessive

Ravaged Dream Series - coming 2023
Forbidden Billionaire Romance
Grumpy Billionaire Boss
Sweetly Forbidden Intern
Dirty Workplace Secret

Dirty royals
Forbidden Royal Romance
The Royal Rebel
The Wicked Prince
His Forbidden Princess
Royal Fake Fiancé

Lyon Dynasty world
Dark Billionaire Romance
King's Capture
Queen's Sacrifice

SINFULLY RICH SERIES
Steamy Billionaire Romance
SINFUL FLING
SINFUL ENEMY
SINFUL BOSS
SINFUL CHANCE
SINFULLY RICH

HIS AND HERS SERIES
HIS BEST FRIEND'S LITTLE SISTER
CLAIMING HER INNOCENCE
HIS TO KEEP
HIS VIRGIN

THE ADDICTION DUET
ADDICTION
OBSESSION

OTHER BOOKS
WILD HEARTS

For more information….
vivian-wood.com
info@vivian-wood.com

www.ingramcontent.com/pod-product-compliance
Lightning Source LLC
Chambersburg PA
CBHW061146210726
48294CB00006B/1601